PLAYING THE
DUTIFUL WIFE

PLAYING THE DUTIFUL WIFE

BY

CAROL MARINELLI

MILLS
BOON®

First published in Great Britain 2013
by Mills & Boon, an imprint of Harlequin (UK) Limited.
Large Print edition 2013
Harlequin (UK) Limited, Eton House,
18-24 Paradise Road, Richmond, Surrey TW9 1SR

© Carol Marinelli 2013

ISBN: 978 0 263 23199 1

Harlequin (UK) policy is to use papers that are natural,
renewable and recyclable products and made from
wood grown in sustainable forests. The logging and
manufacturing process conform to the legal environmental
regulations of the country of origin.

Printed and bound in Great Britain
by CPI Antony Rowe, Chippenham, Wiltshire

CHAPTER ONE

'I'M GOING TO have to go,' Meg said to her mother. 'They've finished boarding, so I'd better turn off my phone.'

'You'll be fine for a while yet.' Ruth Hamilton persisted with their conversation. 'Did you finish up the work for the Evans purchase?'

'Yes.' Meg tried to keep the edge from her voice. She really wanted just to turn off the phone and relax. Meg hated flying. Well, not all of it—just the take-off part. All she wanted to do was close her eyes and listen to music, take some nice calming breaths before the plane prepared for its departure from Sydney Airport—except, as usual, her mother wanted to talk about work. 'Like I said,' Meg said calmly, because if she so much as gave a hint that she was irritated her mum would want to know more, 'everything is up-to-date.'

'Good,' Ruth said, but still she did not leave things there.

Meg coiled a length of her very straight red hair around and around one finger, as she always did when either tense or concentrating.

'You need to make sure that you sleep on the plane, Meg, because you'll be straight into it once you land. You wouldn't believe how many people are here. There are so many opportunities…'

Meg closed her eyes and held on to a sigh of frustration as her mum chatted on about the conference and then moved to travel details. Meg already knew that a car would meet her at Los Angeles airport and take her straight to the hotel where the conference was being held. And, yes, she knew she would have about half an hour to wash and get changed.

Meg's parents were prominent in Sydney's

real estate market and were now looking to branch into overseas investments for some of their clients. They had left for Los Angeles on Friday to network, while Meg caught up with the paperwork backlog at the office before joining them.

Meg knew that she should be far more excited at the prospect of a trip to Los Angeles. Usually she loved visiting new places, and deep down Meg knew that really she had nothing to complain about—she was flying business class and would be staying in the sumptuous hotel where the conference was being held. She would play the part of successful professional, as would her parents.

Even though, in truth, the family business wasn't doing particularly well at the moment.

Her parents were always very eager to jump on the latest get-rich-quick scheme. Meg, who could always be relied on for sensible advice, had suggested that rather than all of them flying over maybe just one of them should go, or perhaps they should give it a miss entirely and concentrate on the properties they already had on their books.

Of course her parents hadn't wanted to hear that. This, they had insisted, was the next big thing.

Meg doubted it.

It wasn't that, though, which caused her disquiet.

Really, when she had suggested that only one of them go—given that she dealt with the legal side of things—Meg had rather hoped they might have considered sending only her.

A week away wasn't just a luxury she required—it was fast becoming a necessity. And it wasn't about the nice hotel—she'd stay in a tent if she had to, just for the break, just for a pause so that she could think properly. Meg felt as if she were suffocating—that wherever she turned her parents were there, simply not giving her room to think. It had been like that for as long as she could remember, and sometimes she felt as if her whole life had been planned out in advance by her parents.

In truth, it probably had.

Meg had little to complain about. She had her own nice flat in Bondi—but, given that she worked twelve-hour days, she never really got to enjoy it, and there was always something at work that needed her attention at weekends: a signature to chase up, a contract to read through. It just never seemed to end.

'We're actually going to look at a couple of properties this afternoon…' Her mum carried on talking as there was a flurry of activity in the aisle beside Meg.

'Well, don't go agreeing to anything until I get there,' Meg warned. 'I mean it, Mum.'

She glanced over and saw that two flight attendants were assisting a gentleman. His face was blocked from Meg's vision by the overhead lockers, but certainly from his physique this man didn't look as if he required assistance.

He was clearly tall and extremely fit-looking, and from what Meg could see he appeared more than capable of putting his own laptop into the overhead locker, yet the attendants danced around him, taking his jacket and offering their apologies as he went to take the seat beside Meg.

As his face came into view Meg, who was already struggling, completely lost her place in the conversation with her mother. The man was absolutely stunning, with very thick, beautifully cut black hair worn just a little too long, so that it flopped over his forehead. He had a very straight Roman nose and high cheekbones. Really, he had all the markings of a *very* good-looking man, but it was his mouth that held her attention—perfectly shaped, like a dark bruise of red in the black of his unshaven jaw, and even though it was a scowling mouth, it was quite simply beautiful.

He threw a brief nod in Meg's direction as he took the seat beside her.

Clearly somebody wasn't very happy!

As he sat down Meg caught his scent—a mixture of expensive cologne and man—and, though she was trying to focus on what her mother was saying, Meg's mind kept wandering to the rather terse conversation that was taking place beside her as the flight attendants did their best to appease a man whom, it would seem, wasn't particularly easy to appease.

'No,' he said to the attendant. 'This will be sorted to my satisfaction as soon as we have taken off.'

He had a deep, low voice that was rich with an accent Meg couldn't quite place. Perhaps Spanish, she thought, but wasn't quite sure.

What she *was* sure of, though, was that he demanded too much of her attention.

Not consciously, of course—she just about carried on talking to her mother, her finger still twirling in her hair—but she could not stop listening to the conversation that was none of her business.

'Once again,' the flight attendant said to him, 'we apologise for any inconvenience, Mr Dos Santos.' Then she turned her attention to Meg, and although friendly and polite, the flight attendant was not quite so gushing as she had so recently been to Meg's fellow passenger. 'You need to turn off your phone, Ms Hamilton. We are about to prepare for take-off.'

'I really do have to go, Mum,' Meg said. 'I'll see you there.' With a sigh of relief she turned off her phone. 'The best part of flying,' she said as she did so—not necessarily to him.

'There is nothing good about flying' came his brusque response as the plane started to taxi towards the runway. Seeing her raised eyebrows, he tempered his words a little. 'At least not today.'

She gave him a small smile and offered a quick 'Sorry,' then looked ahead rather than out of the window. After all he could be in the middle of a family emergency and racing to get somewhere. There could be many reasons for his bad mood and it was none of her business after all.

She was actually quite surprised when he answered her, and when she turned she realised that he was still looking at her. 'Usually I do like flying—I do an awful lot of it—but today there are no seats in first class.'

Niklas Dos Santos watched as she blinked at his explanation. She had very green eyes that were staring right at him. He expected her to give a murmur of sympathy or a small tut tut as to the airline's inefficiency; those were the responses that he was used to, so he was somewhat taken aback at hers.

'Poor you!' She smiled. 'Having to slum it back here in business class.'

'As I said, I fly a lot, and as well as working while flying I need to sleep on the plane—something that is now going to be hard to do. Admittedly I only changed my plans this morning, but even so…' He didn't continue. Niklas thought that was the end of the conversation, that he had explained his dark mood well enough. He hoped that now they could sit in mutual silence, but before he could look away the woman in the seat next to him spoke again.

'Yes, it's *terribly* inconsiderate of them—not to keep a spare seat for you just in case your plans happen to change.'

She smiled as she said it and he understood that she was joking—sort of. She was nothing like anyone he usually dealt with. Normally people revered him, or in the case of a good-looking woman—which she *possibly* was—they came on to him.

He was used to dark-haired, immaculately

groomed women from his home town. Now and then he liked blondes—which she was, sort of. Her hair was a reddish blonde. But, unlike the women he usually went for, there was a complete lack of effort on her part. She was very neatly dressed, in three-quarter-length navy trousers and a cream blouse that was delicate and attractive. Yet the blouse was buttoned rather high and she wore absolutely no make-up. He glanced down to nails that were neat but neither painted nor manicured and, yes, he did check for a ring.

Had the engines not revved then she might have noticed that glance. Had she not looked away at that moment she might have been granted the pleasure of one of his very rare smiles. For she seemed refreshingly unimpressed by him, and Niklas had decided she was not a *possibly* good-looking woman in the least…

But she spoke too much.

He would set the tone now, Niklas decided.

Just ignore her if she spoke again. He had a lot of work to get through during this flight and did not want to be interrupted every five minutes with one of her random thoughts.

Niklas was not the most talkative person—at least he did not waste words speaking about nothing—and he certainly wasn't interested in her assumptions. He just wanted to get to Los Angeles with as much work and sleep behind him as possible. He closed his eyes as the plane hurtled down the runway, yawned, and decided that he would doze till he could turn on his laptop.

And then he heard her breathing.

Loudly.

And it only got louder.

He gritted his teeth at her slight moan as the plane lifted off the runway and turned to shoot her an irritated look—but, given that her eyes were closed, instead he stared. She was actually fascinating to look at: her nose was snubbed, her lips were wide and her eyelashes were a reddish blonde too. But she was incredibly tense, and she was taking huge long breaths that made her possibly the most annoying woman in the world. He could not take it for the next twelve hours, and Niklas decided he would be speaking again to the flight attendant—someone would have to move out of first class.

Simply, this would not do.

Meg breathed in through her nose and then out through her mouth as she concentrated on using her stomach muscles to control her breathing as her 'fear of flying' exercises had told her to do. She twisted her hair over and over, and when that wasn't helping she gripped onto the handrests, worried by the terrible rattling noise above her as the plane continued its less than smooth climb. It really was an incredibly bumpy take-off, and she loathed this part more than anything—could not relax until the flight stewards stood up and the seatbelt signs went off.

As the plane tilted a little to the left Meg's eyes screwed more tightly closed. She moaned again and Niklas, who had been watching her strange actions the whole time, noted not just that her skin had turned white but that there was no colour in her lips.

The minute the signs went off he would speak with the flight attendant. He didn't care if it was a royal family they had tucked in first class; someone was going to have to make room for him! Knowing that he always got his way, and that soon he *would* be moving, Niklas decided that for a moment or two he could afford to be nice.

She was clearly terrified after all.

'You do know that this is the safest mode of transport, don't you?'

'Logically, yes,' she answered with her eyes still closed. 'It just doesn't feel very safe right now.'

'Well, it is,' he said.

'You said that you fly a lot?' She wanted him

to tell her that he flew every single day, that the noise overhead was completely normal and nothing to worry about, preferably that he was in fact a pilot—then she might possibly believe that everything was okay.

'All the time,' came his relaxed response, and it soothed her.

'And that noise?'

'What noise?' He listened for a second or two. 'That's the wheels coming up.'

'No, that one.'

It all sounded completely normal to him, yet Niklas realised *she* probably wasn't quite normal, so he continued to speak to her. 'Today I am flying to Los Angeles, as are you, and in two days' time I will be heading to New York…'

'Then?' Meg asked, because his voice was certainly preferable to her thoughts right now.

'Then I will be flying home to Brazil, where I am hoping to take a couple of weeks off.'

'You're from Brazil?' Her eyes were open now, and as she turned to face him she met his properly for the first time. He had very black eyes that were, right now, simply heaven to look into. 'So you speak…?' Her mind was all scrambled; she could still hear that noise overhead…

'Portuguese,' he said and, as if he was there for her amusement—which for a moment or two longer he guessed he was—he smiled as he offered her a choice. 'Or I can speak French. Or Spanish too, if you prefer…'

'English is fine.'

There was no need to talk any more. He could see the colour coming back to her cheeks and saw her tongue run over pinkening lips. 'We're up,' Niklas said, and at the same time the bell pinged and the flight attendants stood. Meg's internal panic was thankfully over, and he watched as she let out a long breath.

'Sorry about that.' She gave him a rather embarrassed smile. 'I'm not usually that bad, but that really was bumpy.'

It hadn't been bumpy in the least, but he was not going to argue with her, nor get drawn into further conversation. And yet she offered her name.

'I'm Meg, by the way.'

He didn't really want to know her name.

'Meg Hamilton.'

'Niklas.' He gave up that detail reluctantly.

'I really am sorry about that. I'll be fine now. I don't have a problem with flying—it's just take-off that I absolutely loathe.'

'What about landing?'

'Oh, I'm fine with that.'

'Then you have never flown into São Paulo,' Niklas said.

'Is that where you are from?'

He nodded, and then pulled out the menu and started to read it—before remembering that he was going to be moving seats. He pushed his bell to summon the stewardess.

'Is it a busy airport, then?'

He looked over to where Meg sat as if he had forgotten that she was even there, let alone the conversation they had been having.

'Very.' He nodded, and then saw that the flight attendant was approaching with a bottle of champagne. Clearly she must have thought he had rung for a drink—after all, they knew his preferences—but as he opened his mouth to voice his complaint Niklas conceded that it might be a little rude to ask to be moved in front of Meg.

He would have this drink, Niklas decided, and then he would get up and go and have a quiet word with the attendant. Or an angry one if that did not work. He watched as his champagne was poured and then, perhaps aware that her eyes were trained on him, he turned, irritated.

'Did you want a drink as well?'

'Please.' She smiled.

'That is what your bell is for,' he retorted. She didn't seem to realise that he was being sarcastic, so he gave in and, rolling his eyes, ordered another glass. Meg was soon sipping on her beverage.

It tasted delicious, bubbly and icy-cold, and would hopefully halt her nervous chatter—except it didn't. It seemed that a mixture of nerves about flying and the fact that she had never been around someone so drop-dead gorgeous before resulted in her mouth simply not being able to stop.

'It seems wrong to be drinking at ten a.m.' She heard her own voice again and could happily have kicked herself—except then he would perhaps have her certified. Meg simply didn't know what was wrong with her.

Niklas didn't answer. His mind was already back to thinking about work, or rather thinking about all the things he needed to get finalised so that he could actually take some proper time off.

He *was* going to take some time off. He had not stopped for the last six months at the very least, and he was really looking forward to being back in Brazil, the country he loved, to the food he adored and the woman who adored him and who knew how it was…

He would take two or perhaps three weeks, and he was going to use every minute of them indulging in life's simple but expensively pre-pared pleasures—beautiful women and amaz-ing food and then more of the same.

He let out a long breath as he thought about it—a long breath that sounded a lot like a sigh. A bored sigh, even—except how could that be? Niklas asked himself. He had everything a man could want and had worked hard to get it—worked hard to ensure he would never go back to where he had come from.

And he *had* ensured it, Niklas told himself;

he could stop for a little while now. A decent stretch in Brazil would sort this restless feeling out. He thought of the flight home, of the plane landing in São Paulo, and as he did he surprised himself. His champagne was finished. He could get up now and have that word with the flight attendant. But instead Niklas turned and spoke with *her*.

With Meg.

CHAPTER TWO

'SÃO PAULO IS very densely populated.'

They were well over the water now, and she was gazing out at it, but she turned to the sound of his voice and Niklas tried to explain the land that he loved, the mile after mile after mile of never-ending city.

'It is something that is hard to explain unless you have seen it, but as the plane descends you fly over the city for very a long time. Congonhas Airport is located just a couple of miles from downtown...'

He told Meg about the short runway and the difficult approach and the physics of it as she looked at him slightly aghast.

'If the weather is bad I would imagine the captain and crew and most *paulistanos*...' He saw her frown and explained it a little differently. 'If you come from Sao Paulo or know about the airport then you are holding your breath just a little as the plane comes into land.' He smiled at her shocked expression. 'There have been many near-misses—accidents too...'

What a horrible thing to tell her! What a completely inappropriate thing for him to say at this moment! And she had thought him so nice— well, nice-looking at least. 'You're not helping at all!'

'But I am. I have flown in and out of Congonhas Airport more times than I can remember and I'm still here to tell the tale... You really have nothing to worry about.'

'Except that I'm scared of landing now too.'

'Don't waste time in fear,' Niklas said, and then stood to retrieve his computer. He did not usually indulge in idle chatter, and certainly not while flying, but she had been so visibly nervous during take-off, and it had been quite pleasant talking her around. Now she was sitting quietly, staring out of the window, and perhaps he did not have to think about moving seats after all.

The flight steward started to serve some appetizers, and Meg had an inkling that Mr Dos Santos was being treated with some tasty little selections from the first-class menu—because there were a few little treats that certainly weren't on the business class one—and, given that she was sitting next to him, by default Meg was offered them too.

'Wild Iranian caviar on buckwheat blinis, with sour cream and dill,' the flight attendant purred to him, but Niklas was too busy to notice the selection placed in front of him. Instead he was setting up a workstation, and Meg heard his hiss of frustration as he had to move his computer to the side. Clearly he was missing his first-class desk!

'There is no room—' He stopped himself, realising that he sounded like someone who complained all the time. He didn't usually—because he didn't have to. His PA, Carla, ensured that everything ran smoothly in his busy life. But Carla simply hadn't been able to work her magic today, and the fact was between here and LA Niklas had a lot to get done. 'I have a lot of work to do.' He didn't have to justify his dark mood, but he did. 'I have a meeting scheduled an hour after landing. I was hoping to use this time to prepare. It really is inconvenient.'

'You'll have to get your own plane!' Meg teased. 'Keep it on standby...'

'I did!' he said. Meg blinked. 'And for two months or so it was great. I really thought it was the best thing I had ever done. And then...' He shrugged and got back to his laptop, one hand crunching numbers, the other picking all the little pieces of dill off the top of the blinis before eating them.

'And then?' Meg asked, because this man

really was intriguing. He was sort of aloof and then friendly, busy, yet calm, and very pedantic with his dill, Meg thought with a small smile as she watched him continue to pick the pieces off. When the food was to his satisfaction there was something very decadent about the way he ate, his eyes briefly closing as he savoured the delicious taste entering his mouth.

Everything he revealed about himself had Meg wanting to know more, and she was enthralled when he went on to tell her about the mistake of having his own plane.

'And then,' Niklas responded, while still tapping away on his computer, 'I got bored. Same pilot, same flight crew, same chef, same scent of soap in the bathroom. You understand?'

'Not really.'

'As annoying as your chatter may be…' he turned from his screen and gave her a very nice smile '…it is actually rather nice to meet you.'

'It's rather nice to meet you too.' Meg smiled back.

'And if I still had my own plane we would not have met.'

'Nor would we if you were lording it in first class.'

He thought for a moment. 'Correct.' He nodded. 'But now, if you will forgive me, I have to get on with some work.' He moved to do just that, but just before he did he explained further, just in case she had missed the point he was making. 'That is the reason I prefer to fly commercially—it is very easy to allow your world to become too small.'

Now, that part she *did* understand. 'Tell me about it.' Meg sighed.

His shoulders tensed. His fingers hesitated over the keyboard as he waited for her to start up again.

When she inevitably did, he would point out *again* that he was trying to work.

Niklas gritted his teeth and braced himself for her voice—was she going to talk all the way to Los Angeles?

Except she said nothing else.

When still she was quiet Niklas realised that he was actually *wanting* the sound of her voice to continue their conversation. It was at that point he gave up working for a while. He would return to the report later.

Closing his laptop, he turned. 'Tell *me* about it.'

She had no idea of the concession he was making—not a clue that a slice of his time was an expensive gift that very few could afford, no idea how many people would give anything for just ten minutes of his undivided attention.

'Oh, it's nothing…' Meg shrugged. 'Just me feeling sorry for myself.'

'Which must be a hard thing to do with a mouthful of wild Iranian caviar…'

He made her laugh—he really did. Niklas

really wasn't at all chatty, but when he spoke, when he teased, when she met his eyes, there was a little flip in her stomach that she liked the feeling of. It was a thrill that was new to her, and there was more than just something about him...

It was *everything* about the man.

'Here's to slumming it,' Niklas said. They chinked their glasses and he looked into her eyes, and as he did so somehow—not that she would be aware of it—Niklas let her in.

He was a closed person, an extremely guarded man. He had grown up having to be that way— it had meant survival at the time—yet for the first time in far too long he chose to relax, to take some time, to forget about work, to stop for a moment and just be with her.

As they chatted he let the flight steward put his laptop away. They were at the back of business class, tucked away and enjoying their own little world.

The food orders were taken and later served, and Meg thought how nice Niklas was to share a meal with. Food was a passion in waiting for Meg. She rarely had time to cook, and though she ate out often it was pretty much always at the same Italian restaurant where they took clients. They'd chosen different mains, and he smiled to himself at the droop of her face when they were served and she found out that steak tartare was in fact raw.

'It's delicious,' he assured her. 'Or you can have my steak?'

At the back of her mind she had known it was raw, if she'd stopped to think about it, but the menu had been incredibly hard to concentrate on with Niklas sitting beside her, and she had made a rather random selection when the flight steward had approached.

'No, it's fine,' Meg said, looking at the strange little piles of food on her plate. There was a big hill of raw minced steak in the middle, with a raw egg yolk in its shell on the top, surrounded by little hills of onions and capers and things. 'I've always wanted to try it. I just tend to stick to safe. It's good to try different things…'

'It is,' Niklas said. 'I like it like this.'

Something caught in her throat, because he'd made it sound like sex. He picked up her knife and fork, and she watched him pour in the egg, pile on the onions and capers, and then chop and chop again before sliding the mixture through Worcestershire sauce. For a fleeting moment she honestly thought that he might load the fork and feed her, but he put the utensils down and returned to his meal, and Meg found herself breathless and blushing at where her mind had just drifted.

'Good?' Niklas asked when she took her first taste.

'Fantastic,' Meg said. It was nice, not amazing, but made by his hands fantastic it was. 'How's *your* steak?'

He sliced a piece off and lifted the loaded fork and held it to her. This from a man who had reluctantly given her a drink, who had on many occasions turned his back. He was now giving her a taste of food from his plate. He was just being friendly, Meg told herself. She was reading far, far too much into this simple gesture. But as she went to take the fork he lifted it slightly. His black eyes met hers and he moved the fork to her mouth and watched as she opened it. Suddenly she began to wonder if she'd been right the first time.

Maybe he *was* talking about sex.

But if he had been flirting, by the time dessert was cleared it had ended. He read for a bit, and Meg gazed out of the window for a while, until the flight attendant came around and closed the shutters. The lights were lowered and the cabin was dimmed and Meg fiddled with her remote to turn the seat into a bed.

Niklas stood and she glanced up at him. 'Are you off to get your gold pyjamas?'

'And a massage,' Niklas teased back.

She was half asleep when he returned, and watched idly as he took off his tie. Of course the flight attendant rushed to hold it, while another readied his bed, and then he took off his shoes and climbed into the flight bed beside her.

His beautiful face was gone now from her vision, but it was there—right there—in her mind's eye. She was terribly aware of his movements and listened to him turn restlessly a few times. She conceded that maybe he did have a point—the flight bed was more than big enough for Meg to stretch out in, but Niklas was easily a foot taller than her and, as he had stated, he really needed this time to sleep, which must be proving difficult. For Niklas the bed was simply too small, and it was almost a sin that he sleep in those immaculate suit trousers.

She lay there trying not to think about him

and made herself concentrate instead on work—
on the Evans contract she had just completed—
which was surely enough to send her to sleep.
But just as she was closing her eyes, just as she
was starting to think that she might be about
to drift off even with Niklas beside her, she
heard him move again. Her eyes opened and
she blinked as his face appeared over hers. She
met those black eyes, heard again his rich accent, and how could a woman not smile?

'You never did tell me...' Niklas said, smiling as he invited her to join him in after hours
conversation. 'Why is your world too small?'

CHAPTER THREE

THEY PULLED BACK the divider that separated them and lay on their sides, facing each other. Meg knew that this was probably the only time in her life that she'd ever have a man so divine lying on the pillow next to hers, so she was more than happy to forgo sleep for such a glorious cause.

'I work in the family business,' Meg explained.

'Which is?'

'My parents are into real-estate investments. I'm a lawyer...'

He gave a suitably impressed nod, but then frowned, because she didn't seem like a lawyer to him.

'Though I hardly use my training. I do all the paperwork and contracts.'

He saw her roll her eyes.

'I cannot tell you how boring it is.'

'Then why do you do it?'

'Good question. I think it was decided at conception that I would be a lawyer.'

'You don't want to be one?'

It was actually rather hard to admit it. 'I don't think I do…'

He said nothing, just carried on watching her face, waiting for her to share more, and she did.

'I don't think I'm supposed to be one—I mean, I scraped to get the grades I needed at school, held on by my fingernails at university…' She paused as he interrupted.

'You are *never* to say this at an interview.'

'Of course not.' She smiled. 'We're just talking.'

'Good. I'm guessing you were not a little girl who dreamed of being a lawyer?' he checked. 'You did not play with wigs on?' His lips twitched as she smiled. 'You did not line up your dollies and cross-examine them?'

'No.'

'So how did you end up being one?'

'I really don't know where to start.'

He looked at his watch, realised then that perhaps the report simply wasn't going to get done. 'I've got nine hours.'

Niklas made the decision then—they would be entirely devoted to *her.*

'Okay...' Meg thought how best to explain her family to him and chose to start near the beginning. 'In my family you don't get much time to think—even as a little girl there were piano lessons, violin lessons, ballet lessons, tutors. My parents were constantly checking my homework—basically, everything was geared towards me getting into the best school, so that I could get the best grades and go to the best university. Which I did. Except when I got there it was more push, push, push. I just put my head down and carried on working, but now suddenly I'm twenty-four years old and I'm not really sure that I'm where I want to be…' It was very hard to explain it, because from the outside she had a very nice life.

'They demand too much.'

'You don't know that.'

'They don't listen to you.'

'You don't know that either.'

'But I do.' He said. 'Five or six times on the telephone you said, "Mum, I've got to go." Or, "I really have to go now…"' He saw that she was smiling, but she was smiling not at his imitation of her words but because he had been listening to her conversation. While miserable and scowling and ignoring her, he had still been aware. 'You do this.' He held up an imaginary phone and turned it off.

'I can't.' she admitted. 'Is that what you do?'

'Of course.'

He made it sound so simple.

'You say, *I have to go*, and then you do.'

'It's not just that though,' she admitted. 'They want to know everything about my life…'

'Then tell them you don't want to discuss it,' he said. 'If a conversation moves where you don't want it to, you just say so.'

'How?'

'Say, *I don't want to talk about that*,' he suggested.

He made it sound so easy. 'But I don't want to hurt them either—you know how difficult families can be at times.'

'No.' He shook his head. 'There are some advantages to being an orphan, and that is one of them. I get to make my own mistakes.' He said it in such a way that there was no invitation to sympathy—in fact he even gave a small smile, as if letting her know that she did not need to be uncomfortable at his revelation and he took no offence at her casual remark.

'I'm sorry.'

'You don't have to be.'

'But…'

'I don't want to talk about that.' And, far more easily than she, he told her what he was not prepared to discuss. He simply moved the conversation. 'What would you like to do if you could do anything?'

She thought for a moment. 'You're the first person who has ever asked me that.'

'The second,' Niklas corrected. 'I would imagine you have been asking yourself that question an awful lot.'

'Lately I have been,' Meg admitted.

'So, what would you be?'

'A chef.'

And he didn't laugh, didn't tell her that she should know about steak tartare by now, if that was what she wanted to be, and neither did he roll his eyes.

'Why?'

'Because I love cooking.'

'Why?' he asked—not as if he didn't understand how it was possible to love cooking so much, more as if he really wanted her tell him why.

She just stared at him as their minds locked in a strange wrestle.

'When someone eats something I've cooked—I mean properly prepared and cooked...' She still stared at him as she spoke. 'When they close their eyes for a second...' She couldn't properly explain it. 'When you ate those blinis, when you first tasted them, there was a moment...' She watched that mouth move into a smile, just a brief smile of understanding. 'They tasted fantastic?'

'Yes.'

'I wanted to have cooked them.' It was perhaps the best way to describe it. 'I love shopping for food, planning a meal, preparing it, presenting it, serving it...'

'For that moment?'

'Yes.' Meg nodded. 'And I know that I'm good at it because, no matter how dissatisfied my parents were with my grades or my decisions, on a Sunday I'd cook a meal from scratch and it was the one thing I excelled at. Yet it was the one thing they discouraged.'

'Why?' This time he asked because he didn't understand.

'"Why would you want to work in a kitchen?"' It was Meg doing the imitating now. '"Why, after all the opportunities we've given you…?"' Her voice faded for a moment. 'Maybe I should have stood up to them, but it's hard at fourteen…' She gave him a smile. 'It's still hard at twenty-four.'

'If cooking is your passion then I'm sure you would be a brilliant chef. You should do it.'

'I don't know.' She knew she sounded weak, knew she should just say to hell with them, but there was one other thing she had perhaps not explained. 'I love them,' Meg said, and she saw his slight frown. 'They are impossible and over-bearing but I do love them, and I don't want to hurt them—though I know that I'll probably have to.' She gave him a pale smile. 'I'm going to try and work out if I can just hurt them gently.'

After a second or two he smiled back, a pensive smile she did not want, for perhaps he felt sorry for her being weak—though she didn't think she was.

'Do you cook a lot now?'

'Hardly ever.' She shook her head. 'There just never seems to be enough time. But when I do...' She explained to him that on her next weekend off she would prepare the meal she had just eaten for herself and friends...that she would spend hours trying to get it just right. Even if she generally stuck with safer choices, there was so much about food that she wanted to explore.

They lay there, facing each other and talking

about food, which to some might sound boring—but for Meg it was the best conversation she had had in her life.

He told her about a restaurant that he frequented in downtown São Paulo which was famed for its seafood, although he thought it wasn't actually their best dish. When he was there Niklas always ordered their *feijoada*, which was a meat and black bean stew that tasted, he told her, as if angels had prepared it and were feeding it to his soul.

In that moment Meg realised that she had not just one growing passion to contend with, but two, because his gaze was intense and his words were so interesting and she never wanted this journey to end. Didn't want to stop their whispers in the dark.

'How come you speak so many languages?'

'It is good that I do. It means I can take my business to many countries…' He was an international financier, Niklas told her, and then, very unusually for him, he told her a little bit more—which he never, ever did. Not with anyone. Not even, if he could help it, with himself. 'One of the nuns who cared for me when I was a baby spoke only Spanish. By the time I moved from that orphanage…'

'At how old?'

He thought for a moment. 'Three, maybe four. By that time I spoke two languages,' he explained. 'Later I taught myself English, and much later French.'

'How?'

'I had a friend who was English—I asked him to speak only English to me. And I—' He'd been about to say looked for, but he changed it. 'I read English newspapers.'

'What language do you dream in?'

He smiled at her question. 'That depends where I am—where my thoughts are.'

He spent a lot of time in France, he told Meg, especially in the South. Meg asked him where his favourite place in the world was. He was about to answer São Paulo—after all, he was looking forward to going back there, to the fast pace and the stunning women—but he paused for a moment and then gave an answer that surprised even him. He told her about the mountains away from the city, and the rainforests and the rivers and springs there, and that maybe he should think of getting a place there—somewhere private.

And then he thanked her.

'For what?'

'For making me think,' Niklas said. 'I have been thinking of taking some time off just to do more of the same...' He did not mention the clubs and the women and the press that were always chasing him for the latest scandal. 'Maybe I should take a proper break.'

She told him that she too preferred the mountains to the beach, even if she lived in Bondi, and they lay there together and rewrote a vision of her—no longer a chef in a busy international hotel, instead she would run a small bed and breakfast set high in the hills.

And she asked about him too.

Rarely, so rarely did he tell anyone, but for some reason this false night he did—just a little. For some reason he didn't hold back. He just said it. Not all of it, by any means, but he gave more of himself than usual. After all, he would never see her again.

He told her how he had taught himself to read and write, how he had educated himself from newspapers, how the business section had always fascinated him and how easily he had read the figures that seemed to daunt others. And he told her how he loved Brazil—for there you could both work hard and play hard too.

'Can I get you anything Mr Dos Santos…?' Worried that their esteemed passenger was being disturbed, the steward checked that he was okay.

'Nothing.' He did not look up. He just looked at Meg as he spoke. 'If you can leave us, please?'

'Dos Santos?' she repeated when the steward had gone, and he told her that it was a surname often given to orphans.

'It means "from the Saints" in Portuguese,' he explained.

'How were you orphaned?'

'I don't actually know,' Niklas admitted. 'Perhaps I was abandoned, just left at the orphanage. I really don't know.'

'Have you ever tried to find out about your family…?'

He opened his mouth to say that he would rather not discuss it, but instead he gave even more of himself. 'I have,' he admitted. 'It would be nice to know, but it proved impossible. I got Miguel, my lawyer, onto it, but he got nowhere.'

She asked him what it had been like, growing up like that, but she was getting too close and it was not something he chose to share.

He told her so. 'I don't want to speak about that.'

So they talked some more about her, and she could have talked to him for ever—except it was Niklas who got too close now, when he asked if she was in a relationship.

'No.'

'Have you ever been serious about anyone?'

'Not really,' she said, but that wasn't quite true. 'I was about to get engaged,' Meg said. 'I called it off.'

'Why?'

She just lay there.

'Why?' Niklas pushed.

'He got on a bit too well with my parents.' She swallowed. 'A colleague.' He could hear her hesitation to discuss it. 'What we said before about worlds being too small…' Meg said. 'I realised I would be making mine smaller still.'

'Was he upset?'

'Not really.' Meg was honest. 'It wasn't exactly a passionate…' She swallowed. She was *so* not going to discuss this with him.

She should have just said so, but instead she told him that she needed to sleep. The dimmed lights and champagne were starting to catch up with both of them, and almost reluctantly their conversation was closed and finally they slept.

For how long Meg wasn't sure. She just knew that when she woke up she regretted it.

Not the conversation, but ending it, falling asleep and wasting the little time that they had.

She'd woken to the scent of coffee and the hum of the engines and now she looked over to him. He was still asleep, and just as beautiful with his eyes closed. It was almost a privilege to examine such a stunning man more intently. His black hair was swept back, his beautiful mouth relaxed and loose. She looked at his dark spiky lashes and thought of the treasure behind them. She wondered what language he was dreaming in, then watched as his eyes were revealed.

For Niklas it was a pleasure to open his eyes to her.

He had felt the caress of her gaze and now he met it and held it.

'English.' He answered the question she had not voiced, but they both understood. He had been dreaming in English, perhaps about her. And then Niklas did what he always did when he woke to a woman he considered beautiful.

It was a touch more difficult to do so—given the gap between them, given that he could not gather her body and slip her towards him—but the result would certainly be worth the brief effort. He pulled himself up on his elbow and moved till his face was right over her, and looking down.

'You never did finish what you were saying.'
She looked back at him.

'When you said it wasn't passionate...'

She could have turned away from him, could have closed the conversation—his question was inappropriate, really—only nothing felt inappropriate with Niklas. There was nothing that couldn't be said with his breath on her cheek and that sulky, beautiful mouth just inches away.

'I was the one who wasn't passionate.'

'I can't imagine that.'

'Well, I wasn't.'

'Because you didn't want him in the way that you want me?'

Meg knew what he was about to do.

And she wanted, absolutely, for him to do it.

So he did.

It did not feel as if she was kissing a stranger as their lips met—all it felt was sublime.

His lips were surprisingly gentle and moved with hers for a moment, giving her a brief glimpse of false security—for his tongue, when it slipped in, was shockingly direct and intent.

This wasn't a kiss to test the water, and now Meg knew what had been wrong with her from the start, the reason she had been rambling. This thing between them was an attraction so instant that he could have kissed her like this the moment he'd sat down beside her. He could have taken his seat, had her turn off her phone and offered his mouth to her and she would have kissed him right back.

And so she kissed him back now.

There was more passion in his kiss than Meg had ever tasted in her life. She discovered that a kiss could be far more than a simple meeting of lips as his tongue told her exactly what else he would like to do, slipping in and out of her parted lips, soft one minute, rougher the next. Then his hand moved beneath the blanket and stroked her breast through her blouse, so expertly that she ached for more.

Meg's hands were in his hair and his jaw scratched at her skin and his tongue probed a little harder. As she concentrated on that, as she fought with her body not to arch into him, he moved his hand inside her top. Now Niklas became less than subtle with his silent instructions and moved his hand to her back, pulling her forward into his embrace. She swallowed the growl that vibrated from his throat as beneath the blanket he rolled her nipple between his fingers—hard at first, and then with his palm he stroked her more softly.

To the outside world they would appear simply as two lovers kissing, their passion indecent, but hidden. Then Niklas moved over her a little more, so all she could breathe was his scent, and his mouth and his hand worked harder, each subtle stroke making her want the next one even more. Suddenly Meg knew she had to stop this, had to pull back, because just her reaction to his kiss had her feeling as though she might come.

'Come.' His mouth was at her ear now, his word voicing her thought.

'Stop,' she told him, even if it was not what

she wanted him to do, but she could hardly breathe.

'Why?'

'Because,' she answered with his mouth now back over hers, 'it's wrong.'

'But *so* nice.'

He continued to kiss her. Her mouth was wet from his but she closed her lips, because this feeling was too much and he was taking her to the edge. He parted her lips with his tongue and again she tried to close them, clamped her teeth, but he merely carried on until she gave in and opened again to him. He breathed harder, and his hand still worked at her breast, and she was fighting not to gasp, not to moan, to remember where they were as he suckled her tongue.

Meg forced herself not to push his hand far lower, as her body was begging her to do, not to pull him fully on top of her as Niklas made love to her with his mouth.

She hadn't a hope of winning.

He removed his hand from her breast and prised her knotted fingers from his hair. Then he moved her hand beneath his blanket, his body acting as a shield as he held her small hand over his thick, solid length. Her fingers ached to curl and stroke around him, but he did not allow it. Instead he just flattened her palm against him and held it there. His mouth still worked against hers, and she tried to grumble a protest as her hand fought not to stroke, not to feel, not to explore his arousal.

He won.

He smothered her moan with his mouth and sucked, as if swallowing her cry of pleasure, and then, most cruel of all, he loosened his grip on her hand and accepted the dig of her fingers into him. He lifted his head and watched her, a wicked smile on his face, as she struggled to breathe, watched her bite on her lip as he too fought not to come. And he wished the lights were on so he could watch her in colour, wished that they were in his vast bed so the second she'd finished they could resume.

And they would, he decided.

'That,' Niklas said as he crashed back not to earth but to ten thousand feet in the air, 'was the appetiser.'

She'd been right the first time.

He *had* been talking about sex.

She put on a cardigan and excused herself just as the lights came on.

As she stood in the tiny cubicle and examined her face in the mirror she fastened her bra. Her skin was pink from his prolonged attention, her lips swollen, and her eyes glittered with danger. The face that looked back at her was not a woman she knew.

And she was *so* not the woman Niklas had first met.

Not once in her life had she rebelled; never had she even jumped out of her bedroom window and headed out to parties. At university she had studied and worked part-time, getting the grades her parents had expected before following them into the family business. She had always done the right thing, even when it came to her personal relationships.

Niklas had been right. She hadn't wanted her boyfriend in the way she wanted Niklas, and had strung things out for as long as she could before realising she could not get engaged to someone she cared about but didn't actually fancy. She had told her boyfriend that she wouldn't have sex till she was sure they were serious, but the moment he'd started to talk about rings and a future Meg had known it was time to get out.

And *that* was the part that caused her disquiet.

She wasn't the passionate woman Niklas had just met and kissed—she was a virgin, absolutely clueless with men. A few hours off the leash from her parents and she was lying on her back, with a stranger above her and the throb of illicit pulses below. She closed her eyes in shame, and then opened them again and saw the glitter and the shame burned a little less. There was no going back now to the woman she had been, and even if there were she would not change a minute of the time she had spent with Niklas.

She heard a tap against the door and froze for a second. Then she told herself she was being ridiculous. She brushed her teeth and sorted her hair and washed in the tiny sink, trying to brace herself to head back out there.

As she walked down the aisle she noticed her bed had been put away and the seats were up. She attempted polite conversation with Niklas as breakfast was served. He didn't really return her conversation. It was as if what had passed between them simply hadn't happened. He continued to read his paper, dunking his croissant in strong black coffee as if he *hadn't* just rocked her world.

The dishes were cleared and still he kept reading. And as the plane started its descent Meg decided that she now hated landing too—because she didn't want to arrive back at her old life.

Except you couldn't fly for ever. Meg knew that. And a man like Niklas wasn't going to stick around on landing. She knew what happened with men like him, wasn't naïve enough to think it had been anything more than a nice diversion.

She accepted it was just about sex.

And yet it wasn't just the sex that had her hooked on him.

He stretched out his legs, his suit trousers still somehow unrumpled, and she turned away and stared out of the window, trying not to think about what was beneath the cloth, trying not to think about what she had felt beneath her fingers, about the taste of his kisses and the passion she had encountered. Maybe life would have been easier had she not sat next to him—because now everything would be a mere comparison, for even with the little she knew still she was aware that there were not many men like Niklas.

Niklas just continued reading his newspaper, or appeared to be. His busy mind was already at work, cancelling his day. He knew that she would have plans once they landed. That she probably had a car waiting to take her to her hotel and her parents. But he'd think of something to get around that obstacle.

He had no intention of waiting.

Or maybe he would wait. Maybe he'd arrange to meet up with her tonight.

He thought of her controlling parents and turned a page in the paper. He relished the thought of screwing her right under their nose.

She, Niklas decided, was amazing.

There was no *possibly* about it now.

He thought of her face as she came beneath him and shifted just a little in his seat.

'Ladies and gentlemen…' They both looked up as the captain's voice came over the intercom. 'Due to an incident at LAX all planes are now being re-routed. We will be landing in Las Vegas in just over an hour.'

The captain apologised for the inconvenience and they heard the moans and grumbles from other passengers. They felt the shift as the plane started to climb, and had she been sitting next to anyone else Meg might have been complaining too, or panicking about the prolonged flight, or stressing about the car that was waiting for her, or worried about what was going on…

Instead she was smiling when he turned to her.

'Viva Las Vegas,' Niklas said, and picked up her remote, laid her chair flat again and got back to where he had left off.

CHAPTER FOUR

'It was a false alarm.'

They were still sitting on the plane on the tarmac. The second they had landed in Vegas Niklas had pulled out his phone, turned it on and called someone. He was speaking in Portuguese. He had briefly halted his conversation to inform Meg that whatever had happened in Los Angeles had been a false alarm and then carried on talking into his phone.

'Aguarde, por favour!' he said, and then turned again to Meg. 'I am speaking with my PA, Carla. I can ask her to reschedule your flight also. She will get it done quickly, I think.'

And make sure he'd sit next to her too, Niklas decided.

'So?' he asked. 'When do you want to get there?'

Of course the normal response would be as soon as possible, but there was nothing normal about her response to him. Niklas was looking right at her, and there was undoubtedly an invitation in his eyes, but there was something he needed to know—somehow she had to tell him that what had happened between them wasn't usual for her.

To put it mildly.

Except Niklas made her stomach fold into herself, and his eyes were waiting, and his mouth was so beautiful, and she did not want this to end with a kiss at an airport gate. She did not want to spend the rest of her life regretting what would surely be a far more exciting choice than the one she should be making.

He made it for her.

'It sounds as if there is a lot of backlog. The airport will be hell with so many people having to re-route. I could tell her to book our flights for tomorrow.' Niklas had already made the decision. He had not had twenty-four hours to himself in months, had not stopped working in weeks, and right now he could think of no one nicer to escape the world with.

'I'm supposed to be...' She thought of her parents, waiting for her at the conference, waiting for her to arrive, to perform, to work twelve-hour days and accept weekends constantly on call. Hers was a family that had every minute, every week, every year of her life accounted for, and for just for a little while Meg wanted to be able to breathe.

Or rather to struggle to breathe under him as he kissed her and took her breath.

He looked at her mouth as he awaited her answer, watched the finger that twirled in her hair finally pause as she reached her decision, saw her tongue moisten her lips just before she delivered her answer.

'Tomorrow,' Meg said. 'Tell her tomorrow.'

He spoke with Carla for a couple more moments, checked he had the right spelling of her surname and date of birth and passport number, and then clicked off his phone.

'Done.'

She didn't know what his life was like—didn't really understand what the word *done* meant in Niklas Dos Santos's world...

Yet.

They waited for their baggage and she got to kiss him for the first time standing up, got to feel his tall length pressed against her. He loaded their bags onto one trolley and then he did a nice thing, a very unexpected thing: he stopped at one of the shops and bought her flowers.

She smiled as he handed them to her.

'Dinner, breakfast, champagne, kisses, foreplay...' God, he didn't even lower his voice as he handed her the flowers. 'Have I covered everything?'

'You haven't taken me to the movies,' Meg said.

'No...' He shook his head. 'There was a movie on. You chose not to watch it. I cannot be held responsible for that...'

Oh, but he had been. She felt the thorns of the roses press in as he moved closer again and crushed the flowers.

'Consider yourself dated.'

There was no waiting in long queues for Niklas. Customs was a very different thing in his world, and as his hand was holding hers, she too was processed quickly. Suddenly they had cleared Customs and were walking out—and it was then she got her first glimpse of what *done* meant in a world like Niklas's.

Carla must have been busy, for there was already a driver waiting, holding a sign with 'Niklas Dos Santos' written on it. He relieved them of their bags and they followed him to a blacked-out limousine. She never got a glimpse of Vegas as they drove to the hotel, just felt the brief hit of hot desert sun.

No, she never saw Vegas at all.

She was sitting on his lap.

'I'm going to be the most terrible let-down…' She peeled her face from his.

'You're not,' he groaned.

'I am…' God, her head was splitting just at the attempt to be rational. 'Because I have to ring my mum…'

Her hands were shaking as she dialled the number, her mind reeling, because she *had* to tell him she was a virgin. Oh, God, she really was going to be a let-down! His fingers were working the buttons on her trousers now, his hand slipping in and cupping her bum. His mouth was sucking her breast through her blouse as she was connected to her mother, and she heard only smatters of her conversation.

'Yes, I know it was a false alarm…' She tried to sound normal as she spoke with a less than impressed Ruth. 'But all the flights are in chaos and tomorrow was the earliest I could get.' No, she insisted for a third time, there was simply nothing she could do that would get her there sooner. 'I'll call you when I've sorted out a hotel and things. I have to go, Mum, my battery's about to go flat.'

She clicked off the phone and he turned her so that she was sitting astride him. Holding her hips, he pushed her down, so she could feel what would soon be inside her, and for the first time she was just a little bit scared.

'Niklas…'

'Come on…' He did her blouse up. 'We are nearly there.'

She made herself decent, slipped her cardigan over her blouse to hide the wet patch his mouth had made, and found out once again what it was like in his world.

They breezed through check-in, and even their luggage beat them to their huge suite—not that she paid any attention to it, for finally they were alone. As soon as the door shut he kissed her, pushing her onto the bed. He removed his jacket and pulled condoms from his pocket, placing them within reach on the bedside table, and then he removed her trousers, taking her panties with them at the same time.

God, he was animal, and he moaned as he buried his face in her most private of places. Meg felt the purr of his moan, and this new experience coupled with her own arousal terrified her.

'Niklas…' she pleaded as his tongue started to probe. 'When I said my relationship wasn't passionate…'

'We've already proved it had nothing to do with you.' His words were muffled, but he felt her tense and as he looked up he met anxious eyes.

'I haven't done this before.' She saw him frown. 'I haven't done anything.'

There was a rather long pause. 'Good. I will look after you...'

'I know that.'

'I *will*.'

And then his mouth resumed, and she felt his breath in places she had never felt someone breathe before, but still the tension and fear remained. Niklas must have sensed it too, as he raised himself up on his elbows and looked down at her beneath him, her face flushed.

Niklas was a very uninhibited lover; it was the only piece of himself that he readily gave. Sex was both his rest and recreation, and with his usual lovers there was no need for long conversation and coaxing, no need for reticence or taking his time. But as he looked down at her flushed cheeks he recalled their long conversations on the plane, and the enjoyment of spending proper time with another person. He thought of all the things he had told her that he never usually shared with anyone, and he realised he liked not just the woman who lay beneath him but the words that had come from her mouth.

He kissed it now, as if doing so for the first time.

Not their first kiss. Just a gentle kiss—albeit with his erection pressing into her as he thought about what to do.

His first intention had been to push her on the bed and take her quickly, just so that they could start over again, but he really liked her, and he wanted to do this well.

Thoroughly.

Properly.

'I know…'

He sounded as if he'd had an idea, and he stopped kissing her, smiling down at her before rolling off and picking up the phone. He told Meg that a bath would relax her, and as they waited for a maid to come and run it he wrapped her in a vast white dressing gown. She lay on the bed, watching him as he went through his case, and then he joined her on the bed and showed her some documents, his fingers pointing to the pertinent lines, which she read, frowning.

'I don't get this.'

'I had to get a check-up when I was in Sydney, for my insurance…' he explained.

'So?'

'I wasn't worried about the results. I always use protection…' He was so completely matter-of-fact.

'I'm not on the pill,' Meg replied as she understood his meaning, and she saw his eyes widen just a little as she dampened his plans.

'But still…' He stopped himself, shook his head as if to clear it. What the hell had he been thinking? For a second a baby had seemed a minor inconvenience compared to what they might miss out on. He was, Niklas decided, starting to adore her, and that always came with strong warnings attached—that was always his signal to leave.

'Niklas…am I making a big mistake?'

He was as honest with Meg as he was with all women, because his was a heart that would remain closed. 'If you are looking for love, then yes,' Niklas said. 'Because I don't do that.'

'Never?'

'Ever,' Niklas said. He could not bear even the thought of someone depending on him, could not trust himself to provide for another person, just could not envisage sharing, yet alone caring—except already a part of him cared for *her*.

'Then I want as long as we've got,' Meg said.

When the maid left he took her by the hand and led her to the bathroom. The bath was sunken, and as she slid into the water he undressed, and she was looking up at his huge erection, her cheeks paling in colour. Niklas found himself assuring her that nothing would happen between them just yet—not until she was sure she was ready. The need to comfort her and reassure her was a new sensation for him, and as he looked down at her he decided that for the next twenty-four hours he would let himself care.

He climbed into the water with her and washed her slowly, sensually, smoothing the soap over her silky skin. He dunked her head in the water too, just so he could see the red darken.

'Your last boyfriend—did he try...?' Niklas asked as he soaped her arms, curious because he wondered how any man could resist the beautiful woman he held in his arms.

'A bit...' Meg said.

Even her arms blushed, he noted.

'I just...'

'What?' He loved her blushing, and found himself smiling just watching her skin pinken, feeling the warmth beneath his palms as she squirmed.

'I told him I didn't want to do anything like that till we were really serious. You know…'

His eyes widened. 'Married?'

'Engaged,' she corrected.

'Do people really say that?' He sounded incredulous, his soapy hands moving lower, past her breasts and down to her waist. 'How would you know if you wanted to marry someone if you hadn't—?'

'That had nothing to do with it. I wasn't demanding a ring. I realised I was just making up excuses…'

'Because?' He was sliding his soapy hands between her legs now, and she didn't know how to answer. 'Because?' he insisted.

'Because I didn't have any compulsion to sit in a bath with him and let him wash me *there*…' She couldn't believe he expected her to speak as he was doing what he did. 'And then he started talking rings.'

'I bet he did,' Niklas said, because, naked with

her like this, what man wouldn't want his ring on her finger?

Suddenly his brain went to a place it should not, and Niklas tried hard to shut it down. This had to stay as just sex between them. He pulled her straight over to him, hooked her legs over his and kissed her shoulder.

'I loved flying with you…' He said it like a caress as he lifted her hair, and his mouth moved to the back of her neck and sucked hard.

She closed her eyes at the bruise he was making, and then felt his hand move up her thigh. It was his neck she was now kissing, licking away the fragrant water just to get to his skin. As they continued to nip and kiss each other Niklas moved his hand, his finger slipping inside, and when she felt a moment's pain she sucked harder on his neck. He pushed in another finger, stretching her, and again she bit down on his shoulder as pain flashed through her body. She knew he had to stretch her—she had seen that he was huge and this was her first time after all—but he did it with a gentleness that moved her.

He continued to slide his fingers in and out, and then kissed her breast, sucking on her wet nipple. She began to moan and lift herself to his fingers as pleasure washed over her. Niklas realised that things were moving rather faster than he had intended. He wanted her on the bed—or rather they needed to get back to the condoms.

'Come on…' He moved to stand, except her hand found him first and, yes, she deserved a little play too.

He liked being touched by a woman. He had just never expected to enjoy it as much as he did now. Had never expected the naked pleasure in her eyes and the tentative exploration of her hands, just her enjoyment of him, would make him feel as it did.

For enjoy him, Meg did. It was bliss to hold him, huge and slippery and magnificent in her hands, and she was still scared, but rather more excited at the prospect of him being inside her.

'Like this?' she checked, and he closed his eyes and leant his head back on the marble wall behind him.

'Like that,' he said, but then changed his mind. 'Harder.' And he put his hand over hers and showed her—showed her a little too well.

'Come here.' He pulled her up over him. He was seconds away, had to slow down, but he had to have her. He was rubbing himself around her and she was desperate for him to be inside her too.

'We need…' It was him saying it, and he knew he should take her to bed and slip on a condom, but he wanted her this moment, and for once in his life he was conflicted. He knew he could have her now, that he was the only one thinking, and he wanted the pleasure. But as he looked at her, hovering over him, Niklas knew he wouldn't have a hope of pulling out in time.

Her hands were on his shoulders and he was holding her buttocks, almost fighting not to press her down. He wanted to give in, to drive her down and at the same time lift his hips, and he would have—absolutely he would have, in fact—had her phone not rung.

He swore in Portuguese, and then French, and then Spanish at the intrusion.

'Leave it,' he said.

But it rang again, and for a brief moment common sense returned. He stood, taking her wet hand and helping her out as they headed for the bed. He turned off her phone, and checked that his was off too, for he was tired of a world that kept invading his time. Then he looked at the shiny foil packets and realised that the last thing he wanted was to be sheathed when he entered this woman.

'I want to feel you,' he said. 'I want you to feel me.'

And his mind went to a place he never allowed it to go.

He'd been told by plenty of people that he was damaged goods, that a man with his past was not capable of a stable relationship.

Yet he wanted to be stable for a while.

He was tired of the noise and the endless women. Not once had he considered commitment, and he didn't fully now, but surely for a while longer he could carry on caring? He had amassed enough that he could trust himself to take care of another person for a while at least, and if there were consequences to his reckless decision then he could take care of that too.

He could.

In that moment he fully believed that he could.

He would.

No, he did not want others around him today—did not want his thoughts clouded. Usually, to Niklas, rapid thoughts were right, and they were the ones that proved to be the best.

He looked at her, pink and warm and a virgin on his bed, and decided he would do this right.

Thoroughly.

Properly.

'Marry me.'

She laughed.

'I'm serious,' he said. 'That's what people do when they come to Vegas.'

'I think they usually know each other first.'

'I know you.'

'You don't.'

'I know enough,' Niklas said. 'You just don't know me. I *want* to do this.'

And what Niklas Dos Santos wanted he usually got.

'I'm not talking about for ever—I could never settle with one person for very long, or stay in one place—but I can help you sort out the stuff with your family. I can step in so you can step back...'

'Why?' She didn't get it. 'Why would you do that?'

He looked at her for a long time before answering, because she was right. Why *would* he do that? Niklas had had many relationships, many less than emotional encounters, and there had been a couple of long high-maintenance ones. Yet not once in his life had he considered marriage before. Not once had he wanted another person close. He had actually feared that another person might depend on a man who had come from nothing, but as he looked at her for the first time he wasn't daunted by the prospect at all.

Around her—again for the first time—he trusted in himself.

'I like you.'

'But what would you get out of it?'

'You,' he replied, and suddenly it seemed imperative that he marry her—that he make her his even if just for a little while. 'I like sorting things out…and I like you. And…' He gestured to the condoms on the bedside table. 'And I don't like them. So,' he said, reaching for the hotel phone, 'will you marry me?'

There was nothing about him she understood, but more than that there was nothing about herself she understood any more, for in that moment his proposal seemed rather logical.

A solution, in fact.

'Yes.'

He spoke on the phone for just a few moments and then turned and smiled at his bride-to-be.

'Done.'

CHAPTER FIVE

IT WAS THE quickest of quick weddings.

Or maybe not.

They were in Vegas, after all.

Niklas rang down to the concierge and informed them of their plans, telling him how they wanted them executed.

'Do you want them to bring up a selection of dresses?' he asked Meg. 'It's your day; you can have whatever you want.'

'No dress.' Meg smiled.

But there were *some* traditional elements.

He ordered lots of flowers, and they arrived in the room along with champagne, and there was even a wedding cake. Meg sat at a table trying on rings as the celebrant went through the paperwork.

He'd arranged music too, but Niklas chose from a selection already on his phone, and Meg found herself walking at his side to music she didn't know and a man she badly wanted to.

The bride and groom wore white bathrobes, and she stood watching as the titanium ring dotted with diamonds she had chosen was slipped onto her finger. Perhaps bizarrely, there was not a flicker of doubt in her mind as she said yes.

And neither was there a flicker of doubt in Niklas's mind as he kissed his virgin bride and told her that he was happy to be married to a woman he had only met yesterday.

'Today,' Meg corrected and, yes, because of the time difference between Vegas and Australia it *was* still the day they'd first met.

'Sorry to rush you.' He grinned.

There was a mixture of nerves and heady relief when everyone had left.

He undid her robe and took off his, and then he pulled her onto the bed.

'Soon,' Niklas promised as his hands roamed over her, 'you will be wondering how you got through your life without this.'

'I'm wondering now,' Meg admitted, and she wasn't just talking about the sex. She was talking about him too. She had never opened up more fully with another person, had never felt more like herself.

Niklas's kiss was incredibly tender—a kiss she would never have expected from him. He kissed her till she almost relaxed, and then his mouth became more consuming. He needed to shave, but she liked the roughness, liked his naked body wrapped around hers.

She was on her back, and he was on top as he had so badly wanted to be on the plane. He could not wait—not for a moment longer. His knees nudged hers apart and he slipped his fingers briefly in, checking she was ready for him, finding that she was.

And now there was nothing between them.

And he was no longer patient.

He warned her it would hurt.

He watched her face as she blanched in pain, then kissed her hard on the mouth.

As he drove into her she screamed into his mouth, because that first thrust seemed to go on for ever, and every part of her felt as if it was tearing just to accommodate his long, thick length. He tried to be gentle, but he was too large for that. But once he had ripped off that Band-Aid he kept moving within her, kept on kissing her mouth, her face, giving her no choice but to grow accustomed to the new sensations she was feeling. He moved within her as his tongue had earlier described that he would, moving deep till he had driven her wild. He wasn't kissing her now, and she looked up to see his face etched with concentration, his eyes closed, his body moving rapidly as hers rose to meet him.

Now it was Meg's hands urging him on, digging her fingers into his tight buttocks, whimpering as she sought relief, and then he opened his eyes and let her have it, spilled every last drop deep into her. Her orgasm followed quickly after, and she was frenzied as she came, almost scared at the power of her body's response, at the things he had taught her to do.

And then he collapsed on top of her, his breathing heavy, and although it felt like a dream somehow it was real. Meg realised that he had been right—she had no idea how she'd got through her life without this.

Without him.

'Shouldn't we be regretting this by now?' Meg asked.

They were lying in a very rumpled bed and it was morning. Her body ached with the most delicious hurt, but Niklas had assured her for this morning's lesson she would need only her mouth.

'What's to regret?' He turned on the bed and looked over to her.

He didn't do happiness, but he felt the first rays of it today. He liked waking up to her, and the rest was mere detail that he would soon sort out.

'You live in Brazil and I live in Australia...'

'As we both know, there are planes...' He looked across the pillow. 'Do you worry about everything?'

'No.'

'I think you do.'

'I don't.'

'So how shall we tell your parents?'

He saw her slight grimace.

'They might be pleased for you.'

As the real world invaded so too did confusion. 'I doubt it. It will be a terrible shock.' She thought for a moment. 'I think once they get used to the idea they'll be pleased.' And then she swallowed nervously. 'I *think*.'

He smiled at her worried face. 'First of all *you* need to get used to the idea.'

'I don't know much about you.'

'There isn't much to know,' Niklas said.

She rather doubted that.

'I don't have family, as I said, so you have avoided having a mother-in-law. I hear from friends they can sometimes be a problem, so that's an unexpected bonus for you!'

He could be so flippant about things that were important, Meg thought, and there was so much she wanted to find out about him. She wondered how he had survived without a family, for a start, how he had made such a success of himself from nothing—because clearly he had. But unlike their wedding some things, Meg guessed, had to be taken more slowly—she couldn't just sit up and fire a thousand questions at him. Somehow she knew it wasn't something he would talk about easily, but she tried. 'What was it like, though?' Meg asked. 'Growing up in an orphanage?'

'There were many orphanages,' he said. 'I was moved around a lot.' Perhaps he realised he wasn't answering her question, because he added, 'I don't know, really. I try not to think about it.'

'But…'

He halted her. 'We're married Meg. But that doesn't mean we need every piece of each other. Let's just enjoy what we have, huh?'

So if he didn't want to talk about himself she'd start with the easier stuff instead. 'You live in São Paulo?'

'I have an apartment there,' Niklas said. 'If I am working in Europe I tend to stay at my house in Villefranche-sur-Mer. And now I guess I'll have to look for somewhere in Sydney…' His smile was wicked. 'If your father gets really cross, maybe I can ask if he knows any good houses—if he would be able to help…'

Meg started to laugh, because it sounded as if he did understand where she was coming from. Niklas was right—a nice big commission would certainly go a long way towards appeasing her father. She realised that the shock would wear off eventually, and that her rather shallow parents would be delighted to find somewhere for their rich new son-in-law to live.

As Meg lay there, and the sun started to work its way through the chink in the curtains, she started to realise that this was the happiest she had been in her life. But even with that knowledge there was one part about last night that had been unjustifiably reckless.

'I'll go on the pill...' she said. 'If it isn't already too late.'

He had said this wasn't for ever, and the wedding ring that had seemed a solution yesterday was less than one now.

'If last night brings far-reaching consequences you will both be taken care of.'

'For a while?'

He looked over and knew that, unlike most women, Meg wasn't talking about money. But his bank account was the only thing not tainted by his past.

'For a while,' Niklas said. 'I promise you— we'll be arguing within weeks, we'll be driving each other insane—and not with lust…' He smiled in all the wrong places, but he made her smile back. 'You'll be glad to see the back of me.'

She doubted it.

'I'm hard work,' he warned.

But worth it.

Though she *was* going on the pill.

And then he looked over to her again, and for as long as it was like this she could adore him.

'I am going to write to the airline tomorrow and thank them for not having a first-class seat,' he said.

'I might write and thank them too.'

'It will be okay,' he told her. 'Soon I will ring

Carla and I will have her re-schedule things. Then we will meet with your parents and I will tell them.' He grinned at her horrified expression.

'*I'll* speak to my parents.'

'No,' Niklas said. 'Because you will start apologising and doubting and I am a better negotiator.'

'Negotiator?'

'How long do you want off for our honeymoon?' Niklas said. 'Of course you will want to give them notice—you don't want to just walk out—but for now we should have some time together. Maybe I'll take you to the mountains...' There was no gap between them now, so he pulled her across. 'And I will also tell them that we will have a big wedding in a few weeks.'

'I'm happy with the wedding we had.'

'Don't you want a big one?'

Her hand slid down beneath the sheet and she loved it that he laughed, not understanding that laughter was actually rare for him. Then her mouth followed her hands, and he lay there as she inexpertly woke another part of him.

'Don't you want a proper wedding, with family and dancing?'

'I hate dancing…' She kissed all the way down his length and she felt his hand in her hair, gently lifting her to where he wanted more attention.

'I do too.'

'I thought all Brazilians could dance?'

'Stop talking,' Niklas said. 'And I never said I couldn't. I just don't.'

She looked up at the most stunning, complicated man who had ever graced her vision and thought of his prowess and the movement of his body. All of it had been for her, and she shivered at the thought of the days and nights to come, of getting to know more and more of him. Already she knew that she was starting to want for ever, but that wasn't what this was about.

And then she tasted him again.

His hands moved her head as he promised she

would not hurt him and told her exactly what to do with her mouth. She was lost in his scent, the feel of him in her mouth, and the shock of his rapid come was a most pleasant surprise. It was a surprise for Niklas too, but this was how she moved him.

He did not want to get out of bed—did not want to get back to the world. Except no doubt it was screaming for him by now—he had never had his phone turned off for so long.

He climbed out of bed and she lay there, just staring at the ceiling, lost in thoughts of him and the time they would take to get to know the other properly.

And Niklas was thinking the same. He had been looking forward to some time off, had been aware that he needed some, now he could not wait to take it.

He showered quickly and considered shaving, and then he picked up his phone, impatient to speak to Carla, to change his plans yet again. He grimaced when he saw how many missed calls he'd had, how many texts, and then he frowned—because there were hundreds. From Carla, from Miguel, from just about everyone he knew…

It was his first inkling that something was wrong.

Niklas had no family, and the only person he had ever really cared about was in bed in the next room, so he didn't have any flare of panic, but there was clearly a problem. Problems he was used to, and was very good at sorting them out.

It just might take a little time, that was all, when really he would far rather be heading back to bed. He dialled Carla's number, wondering if he should tell Meg to order some breakfast. He would just as soon as he made this call.

She could hear him in the lounge, speaking in his own language into his phone. She lay there for ages, twisting her new ring around her finger. Then, as he still spoke on the phone, she realised she wasn't actually terrified at the prospect of telling her parents, and even if this wasn't the most conventional of marriages, even if he had warned her it would end some day, she was completely at peace with what had occurred.

The only thing she was right now, Meg realised, was starving.

'I'm going to ring for breakfast,' she said as he walked back into the room, and then she looked over and frowned, because even though he had been gone ages she was surprised to see that he was dressed.

'I have to return to Brazil.'

'Oh.' She sat up in the bed. 'Now?'

'Now.'

He was not looking at her, Meg realised. What she did not realise was that precisely two seconds from now he was going to break her heart.

'We made a mistake.'

As easily as that he did it.

'Sorry?'

'The party's over.'

'Hold on…' She was completely sideswiped. 'What happened between there and here?' She pointed to the lounge he had come from. 'Who changed your mind?'

'I did.'

'What? Did you suddenly remember you had a fiancée?' Meg shouted. 'Or a girlfriend…?' She was starting to cry. 'Or five kids and a wife…?' It was starting to hit home how little she knew about him.

'There's no wife…' he shrugged '…except you. I will speak with my legal team as soon as I return to Brazil, see if we can get it annulled. But I doubt it…'

He didn't even sit on the bed to tell her it was over, and she realised what a fool she had been, how easily he had taken her in.

'If it cannot be annulled they will contact you

for a divorce. I'll make a one-off settlement,' he said.

'Settlement?'

'My people will sort it. You can fight me for more if you choose, but I strongly suggest that you quickly accept. Of course if you are pregnant…'

He stood there with the sun streaming through the curtains behind him, and all she could see was the dark outline of a man she didn't know.

'It might be a good idea to think about the morning-after pill.'

And then there was a knock on the door and it was a bellboy to take his case.

'I've asked for a late check-out for you, if you want to reschedule your flight. Have breakfast…' he offered, as if this was normal, and then he tipped the bellboy, who left with his luggage.

'I don't understand…' She was turning into

some hysterical female, sitting screaming on a bed as her one-night stand walked off.

'This is the type of thing people do in Vegas. We had fun…'

'Fun!' She couldn't believe what she was hearing.

'It's no big deal.'

'But it is for me.'

'It's about time that you grew up, then.'

She had never expected him to be cruel, but she had no idea what she was dealing with. Niklas could be cruel when necessary, and today it was.

Very necessary.

He could not look at her. She was sitting on the bed in tears, pleading with him, and also, he noted, growing increasingly angry. Her voice rose as she told him that *he* was the one who needed to grow up, that *he* was the one who needed to sort out his life, and her hands were waving. Any minute now he thought she would rise and attack him. He wanted to catch her wrists and kiss the fear away, wanted to feel just for a moment her body writhing in anger and to reassure her—except he had nothing he could reassure her with. He knew how bad things would be shortly, so he had to be cruel to be kind.

'What did you have to marry me for?' she shouted. 'I was clearly already going to sleep with you...'

She was about to lunge at him, Niklas knew. She was kneeling on the bed, still grabbing the sheet around her for now, but in a moment it would be off. Her green eyes were flashing, her teeth bared and with his next words he knew he would end this.

'I told you yesterday.' He went to the bedside and flicked a few foil packets to the floor. 'I don't like condoms.'

He took the clawing to his cheek, stood there as she sprang towards him, then caught and held her naked fury by the arms for a moment. And then he pushed her back on the bed.

And as simply as that he was gone.

A minute ago the only things on her mind had been breakfast and making love with her new husband.

Now they were talking annulments and settlements.

Or rather they weren't talking.

He was gone.

He had left with cruel words and livid scratches on his cheek and she just lay there, reeling, her anger like a weight that did not propel her, but instead seemed to pin her down to the bed. It was actually an achievement to breathe.

A few minutes later Meg realised she was breathing in through her nose and out through her mouth, as she had done on the plane during take-off. Her own body was rallying to bring her out from the panic she now found herself in. Still she lay there and tried to make sense of something there was no sense to be made of.

He had played her.

Right from the start it had all been just a game to him.

Except this was her life.

Maybe he was right. Maybe she did need to grow up. If a man like Niklas could so easily manipulate her, could have her believing in love at first sight, then maybe she *did* need to sort herself out. She curled into herself for a moment, breathed for a bit, cried for a bit, and then, because she had to, Meg stood.

She didn't have breakfast.

She ordered coffee instead, and gulped on the hot sweet liquid in the hope that it would warm her, would wean her brain out of its shock. It did not.

She showered, blasting her bruised, tender body with water, for she could not bear to step into the bath where they had kissed and so nearly made love.

Sex, Meg reminded herself. Because as it turned out love at first sight had had nothing to do with it.

She dressed quickly, unable to bear being in a room that smelt of them, and then she looked at the rumpled and bloodstained sheet on the bed where he had taken her and thought she might throw up.

Within an hour she was at the airport.

And just a little while later she was sitting on a plane and trying to work out how to get her life back to where it had been yesterday.

Except her heart felt as bruised and aching as the most intimate parts of her body, and her eyes, swollen from crying, felt the same.

Meg ordered a cool eye mask from the attendant. Before putting it on she slid off her wedding ring and put it on a chain around her neck, trying to fathom what had happened.

She couldn't.

She did her best with make-up in the toilet cubicle just before they came in for landing. She lifted her hair and saw the bruise his mouth had left on her neck and felt a scream building that somehow she had to contain. She covered her eyes with sunglasses and wondered how she would ever get through the next few hours, days, weeks.

'Thank God...' Her mum met her at the baggage carousel. 'The car's waiting. I'll bring you up to speed on the way.' She peered at her daughter. 'Are you okay?'

'Just tired,' Meg answered, and then she looked at her mum and knew she could never, ever tell her, so instead she forced a smile. 'But I'm fine.'

'Good,' said her mum as they grabbed her case and headed for the car. 'How was Vegas?'

CHAPTER SIX

MEG STOOD IN her office, looking out of the window, her fingers, as they so often did, idly turning the ring that still, almost a year later, lived on a chain around her neck.

She wasn't looking forward to tonight, given what she had to tell her parents.

It had nothing to do with Niklas. There had been eleven months of no contact now. Eleven months for Meg to start healing. Yet still she didn't know how to start.

She couldn't bear to think about him, let alone tell anyone what had happened.

And even though she could not bear to think about him, even though it actually hurt to do so, of course all too often Meg did.

It hurt to remember the good bits.

The bad bits almost killed her.

Surprisingly, she couldn't quite work out if she regretted it.

Niklas Dos Santos, for the brief time he had appeared in it, had actually changed her life. Meeting him had changed her. Hell *did* make you stronger. This was her life and she must live it, and Meg had decided that she was finally going to follow her dreams and study to be a chef. Now she just had to tell her parents. So in a way tonight did in fact have something to do with him.

The strange thing was, she wanted to tell Niklas about her decision too—was fighting with herself not to contact him.

As painful as it was to remember, as brutal as his departure had been, still a part of her was grateful for the biggest mistake of her life and, fiddling with his ring as she so often did, Meg felt tears sting her eyes.

That was the only thing that was different today.

She hadn't cried for him since that morning. Actually, she had, but it had only been the once—the morning a couple of weeks later when she had got her period. Meg had sunk to her knees and wept on the toilet floor, not with relief, but because there was nothing left of them.

Nothing to tell him.

No reason for contact.

Apart from the paperwork it was as over as it could be.

So for the best part of a year she had completely avoided it. Had tried not to think of him while finding it impossible not to.

Every day had her waiting for a thick legal letter with a Brazilian postmark and yet it had never arrived.

Every night was just a fight not to think.

Sometimes Meg was tempted to look him up

on the internet and find out more about the man who she could not forget—yet she was scared to, scared that even a glimpse of his face on her computer screen would have her picking up the phone to beg.

That was how much she still missed him.

Sometimes she grew angry, and wanted to contact him so that they could initiate the divorce, but that would be just an excuse to ring him. Meg knew she didn't need to speak with him to divorce him, yet she had not even started the simple process, because once she started down that path it would stop being a dream—which sometimes she thought it must have been...

Then her fingers would move to the cool metal of his ring and she'd find out again it was real.

She looked up at the clock and saw that it was time for lunch. Grateful for the chance of some fresh air while she worked out exactly how to tell her parents she was leaving the family business, Meg was tempted to ignore the ringing phone.

She wished she had when she answered it, because some new clients had arrived and were insisting that they be seen immediately.

'Not without an appointment.' Meg shook her head. She was fed up with pushy clients and the continual access she was expected to provide. 'I'm going to lunch.'

'I've told them that you're about to go for lunch.' Helen sounded flustered. 'But they said that they would wait till you get back. They are adamant that they see you today.'

Meg was sick of that word—everyone was *adamant* these days, and because there wasn't much work around her parents insisted more and more that they must jump to potential clients' unreasonable demands.

'Just tell them that they need to book,' Meg said, but as she went to end the call she froze when she heard a certain name.

A name that had her blood running simultaneously hot and cold.

Cold because she had dreaded this day—dreaded their worlds colliding, dreaded the one mistake in her crafted life coming back to haunt her—but at the same time hot for the memories the name Dos Santos triggered.

'He's here?' Meg croaked. 'Niklas is here?'

'No,' Helen answered, and Meg was frustrated at her own disappointment when she heard that it wasn't him. 'It's *regarding* a Mr Dos Santos, apparently, and these people really are insistent...'

'Tell them to give me a moment.'

She needed that moment. Meg really did.

She sank into her chair and poured a drink of water, willed herself to calm down, and then she checked her appearance in the mirror that she kept in her drawer. Her hair was neatly tied back and though her face was a touch pale she looked fairly composed—except Meg could see her own eyes were darting with fear.

There was nothing to fear, Meg told herself. It wasn't trouble that had arrived. It had been almost a year after all. No doubt his legal team were here to get her signature on divorce papers. She closed her eyes and tried to calm herself, but it didn't help because all she could see was herself and Niklas, a tangle of legs and arms on a bed, and the man who had taken her heart with him when he left. Now it really was coming to an end.

She stood as Helen brought her visitors in and sorted out chairs for them. Then Helen offered water or coffee, which all three politely declined, and finally, when Helen had left and the door was closed, Meg addressed them.

'You wanted to see me?'

'First we should introduce ourselves.'

A well-spoken gentleman started things off. He introduced himself and his colleague and then Rosa, a woman whom Meg thought might be around forty, took over. It was terribly difficult to tell her age. She was incredibly elegant, her make-up and hair completely immaculate, her voice as richly accented as Niklas's had been, and it hurt to hear the familiar tone—familiar because it played over and over each night in her dreams. But she tried not to think of that, tried to concentrate on Rosa as she told Meg that they worked at the legal firm Mr Dos Santos used. She went through their qualifications and their business structure, and as she did so Meg felt her own qualifications dissolve beneath her—these were high-end lawyers and clearly here to do business. But Meg still didn't understand why Niklas had felt it necessary to fly three of his most powerful lawyers all the way to Australia, simply to oversee their divorce.

A letter would have sufficed.

'First and foremost,' Rosa started, 'before we go any further, we ask for discretion.'

They were possibly the sweetest words that Meg could hope to hear in this situation.

'Of course' was her response, but that wasn't enough for Rosa.

'We *insist* on your absolute discretion,' Rosa reiterated, and for the first time Meg felt her hackles rise.

'I would need to know what you're here in regard to before I can make an assurance like that.'

'You are married to Niklas Dos Santos?'

'I think we all know that,' Meg said carefully.

'And do you know that your husband is facing serious charges of embezzlement and fraud?'

Ice slid down her spine. Her hackles were definitely up now, and Meg thought for a moment before answering, 'I had no idea.'

'If he is found guilty he will probably never be released.'

Meg ran her tongue over her lips and tasted the wax of the lipstick she had applied earlier. She could feel beads of sweat breaking out on her forehead and felt nauseous at the very thought of a man like Niklas confined and constricted. She felt sick, too, at the thought of what he must have done to face serving life behind bars.

'He is innocent.' The man who had first introduced them spoke then, and Meg couldn't help raising one of her eyebrows, but she made no comment.

Of course his own people would say that he was innocent.

They were his lawyers after all.

She didn't look at Rosa when she spoke. Instead she examined her nails, tried incredibly hard to stop her fingers from reaching for her hair. She did not want to give them any hint that she was nervous.

'We believe that Niklas is being set up.'

What else would they say? Meg thought.

'I really don't see what this has to do with me.' Meg looked in turn at each of the unmoved faces and was impressed by her own voice when

she spoke. She possibly sounded like a lawyer, or a woman in control, though of course
inside she was not. 'We were married for less
than twenty-four hours and then Niklas decided
that it was a mistake. Clearly he was right. We
hardly knew each other. I had no idea about any
of his business affairs. Nothing like that was
ever discussed...'

Rosa spoke over her. 'We believe that Niklas
is being set up by the head of our firm.'

It was then that Meg started to realise the
gravity of the situation. These people were not
just defending their client, they were implicating their own principal.

'We have had little access to the case, which
in something as big as this is unusual, and without access to the evidence we cannot supply
a rigorous defence. For reasons we cannot yet
work out, we believe Miguel is intending to
misrepresent Niklas. Of course we cannot let
our boss know that we suspect him. He is the

only one who has access to Niklas while he is being held awaiting a trial date.'

'He's in prison now?'

'He has been for months.'

Meg reached for her water but her glass was empty. Her hands were shaking as she refilled it from the jug. She could not stand the thought of him locked up, could not bear to think of him in prison, did not want those thoughts haunting her. She didn't like the new nightmares these people had brought, and she wanted them gone now.

'It really is appalling, but...' She didn't know how she could help them—didn't know the Brazilian legal system, just didn't know why they were here. 'I don't see how it has anything to do with me. As I said, I'm not involved in his business...' And then she started to panic, because maybe as his wife she had a different involvement with Niklas that they were here to discuss.

'We have made an application of behalf of Niklas for him to exercise his conjugal rights...'

Meg could hear her own pulse pounding in her ears as Rosa continued speaking and she drained her second glass of water. Her throat was still impossibly dry. Her fingers moved to her hair and she twirled the strand around one finger, over and over.

'Niklas is entitled to one phone call a week and a two-hour conjugal visit once every three weeks. He is being brought before the judge in a fortnight for the trial date to be set and we need you to fly there. At your visit with him on Thursday you are to tell him that only when he is in front of the judge he is to fire his lawyer. Before that he is to give no hint. Once he has fired Miguel we will step in for him.'

'No.' Meg shook her head and pulled her finger out of her hair. She was certain of her answer, did not need to think about this for a moment. She just wanted them gone.

'The only way we can get in contact with him is through his wife.'

'I'll phone him.' It was the most she would do. 'You said that he was entitled to a weekly phone call...' And then she shook her head again, because of course the calls would be monitored. 'I can't see him.' She could not. 'We were married for twenty-four hours.'

'Correct me if I am wrong...' Rosa was as tough with the truth as she was direct. 'According to the records we have found you have been married for almost a year.'

'Yes, but we—'

'There has been no divorce?'

'No.'

'And if Niklas was dead and I was here bringing you a cheque would you hand it back and say, *No, we were only married for twenty-four hours?* Would you say, *No, give this to someone else. He had nothing to do with me...?*'

Meg's face was red as she fought for an answer, but she did not know that truth—not that it stopped Rosa.

'And because you have not screamed annulment I am assuming consensual sex occurred.'

Meg felt her face grow redder, because sex had been the only thing they had had between them.

'If you had found yourself pregnant, would you not have contacted him? Would you have told yourself it did not count as you were only married for twenty-four hours? Would you have told your child the same…?'

'You're not being fair.'

'Neither is the system being fair to my client,' Rosa said. 'Your husband will be convicted of a crime he did not commit if you do not get this message to him.'

'So I'm supposed to fly to Brazil and sit in some trailer or cell and pretend that we're…?'

'There will be no pretending—you *will* have sex with him,' Rosa said. 'I don't think you understand what is at stake here, and I don't think you understand the risks to Niklas and his case if it is discovered that we are trying to get information in. There will be suspicions if the bed and the bin...'

Thankfully she did not go into further detail, but it was enough to have Meg shake her head.

'I've heard enough, thank you. I will start preparing the paperwork for divorce today.' She stood.

They did not.

'Marrying Niklas was the biggest mistake of my life,' Meg stated. 'I have no intention of revisiting it and I'm certainly not...' She shook her head. 'No. We were a mistake.'

'Niklas never makes mistakes,' Rosa countered. 'That is why we know he is innocent. That is why we have been working behind our own principal's back to ensure justice for him.' She looked to Meg. 'You are his only chance, and whether or not it is pleasant, whether or not you feel it is beneath you, this *must* happen.'

She handed her an envelope and Meg opened it to find an itinerary and airline tickets.

'There is a flight booked for you tomorrow night.'

'I have a life,' Meg flared. 'A job, commitments…'

'A visit has been approved for Thursday. It is the only chance to make contact with him before the pre-trial hearing in two weeks' time. After you have seen him you can go to Hawaii—though we might need you to go back for another visit in three weeks, if things don't go well.'

'No.' How else could she say it? 'I won't do it.'

Rosa remained unmoved. 'You may want this all to go away, but it cannot. Niklas deserves this chance and he will get it. You will see, when you check your bank account, that you are being well compensated for your time.'

'Excuse me?' Meg was furious. 'How dare you? How on earth did you…?' But it wasn't about how they had found out her bank details. It wasn't that that was the problem right now. 'It's not about money...'

'So it's the morality of it, then?' Rosa questioned. 'You're too precious to sleep with your own husband even it means he has to spend the rest of his life behind bars?'

Rosa made it sound so simple.

'For the biggest mistake of your life, you chose rather well, did you not?' Rosa sneered. 'You are being paid to sleep with Niklas—it's hardly a hardship.'

Meg met her eyes and was positive that he and Rosa had slept together. They both stared for a moment, lost in their own private thoughts. Then Rosa stood, a curl on her lip, and another sassy Brazilian gave her opinion of Meg as she upended her life.

'You need to get over yourself.'

CHAPTER SEVEN

WHEN THEY HAD gone, Meg did what she had spent a year avoiding.

She looked up the man she had married and found out just how powerful he was—or had been before he had been charged. She understood now that the Niklas Dos Santos she was reading about would be less than impressed to find himself in business class. And then she read about the shock his arrest had caused. Niklas might have a reputation in business as being ruthless, but he had always seemed honest—which was apparently why it had made it so easy for him to con some high-flying people into parting with millions. They had believed the lies that had been told to them. His business peers' trust in him had made them gullible, and despite Rosa's and her colleagues' protestations of his innocence, for Meg the articles cast doubt.

She knew, after all, how effortlessly he had read *her*, how easily he had played *her*. Meg had seen another side to Niklas and it wasn't one she liked.

And yet, as Rosa had pointed out, he was her husband, and she was apparently his one hope of receiving a fair trial.

And then Meg clicked on images and wished she had not.

The first one she saw was of him handcuffed and being bundled into a police car.

There were many more of Niklas, but they were not of the man she knew. The suit was on and the tie was beautifully knotted, the hair was as she remembered, but not in one single image did she see him smiling or laughing. Not one single picture captured the Niklas she had so briefly known.

And then she found another image—one that proved the most painful of all to see.

His arrogant face was scowling, there were three scratches on his cheek that her nails had left there, and a deep bruise on his neck that her mouth had made. Meg read the headline: *Dos Santos vira outra mulher!* Meg clicked for a translation. She wanted to know if he had returned that morning and been arrested—wanted to know if that was the reason he had been so cruel to her. Had he known he was about to be arrested and ended it to protect her? She waited for the translation to confirm it, held her breath as it appeared: *Dos Santos upsets another woman!*

And even in prison, even locked up and a world away, somehow he broke her heart again.

There was a knock at the door. Her mother didn't wait for an answer, just opened it and came in. 'Helen said you had visitors?'

'I did.'

'Who were they?'

'Friends.'

She saw her mum purse her lips and knew she would not leave until she found out who her friends were and what they wanted. Even without the arrival of her visitors Meg remembered she had been due for a difficult conversation with her parents today, and now seemed like a good time to get it over with.

'Can you get Dad…?' Meg gave her mum a pale smile. 'I need to speak to you both.'

It didn't go well.

'After all we've done for you' was the running theme, and the words Meg had expected to hear when she told them that she had chosen not to continue working in the family firm.

She didn't mention Niklas. It was enough for them to take in without giving them the added bonus of a son-in-law! And one in prison too.

It should have been a far harder conversation

to have, yet she felt as if all her emotions and fears were reserved for the decision that was still to come, and Meg sat through the difficult conversation with her parents pale and upset, but somehow detached.

'Why would you want to be a chef?' Her mother simply didn't get it—didn't get that her daughter could possibly want something that had not been chosen for her. 'You're a lawyer, for God's sake, and you want to go and work in some kitchen—?'

'I don't know exactly what I want to do,' Meg broke in. 'I don't even know if I'll be accepted…'

'Then why would you give it all up?'

And she didn't know how to answer—didn't know how to tell them that she didn't feel as if she was actually giving up *anything*, that she was instead taking back her life.

Just not yet.

She told them she was taking a holiday, though

she still wasn't sure that she was, but even without Niklas looming large in her thoughts taking a few weeks off while her parents calmed down seemed sensible.

'And then I'll come back and work for a couple of months,' Meg said. 'I'm not going to just up and leave...'

But according to her parents she already had.

Later, as she sat on the balcony of her small flat and looked at the stunning view, Meg thought about her day. What should have been a difficult conversation with her parents, what should have her sitting at home racked with guilt and wondering if she'd handled things right, barely entered her thoughts now. Instead she focused on the more pressing problem looming ahead.

Quietly she sat and examined the three things she had that proved her relationship with Niklas had actually existed.

She took the ring from the chain around her neck and remembered the certainty she had felt when he had slipped it on—even though he had told her it could never be for ever, somehow she had felt it was right.

And then she picked up the marriage certificate she had retrieved from her bedside table and examined the dark scrawl of his signature. *Niklas Dos Santos.* She saw the full stop at the end of his name and could even hear the sound his pen had made as he'd dotted the document.

Finalised it.

And then she examined the third thing, the most painful thing—a heart that even eleven months on was still exquisitely tender.

There had been no one since, no thought of another man since that time. She felt dizzy as she peered into her feelings, scared as to what she might find. The truth was there waiting and she hadn't wanted to see it. It hurt too much to admit it.

She loved him.

Or rather she had.

Absolutely she had, or she would never have married him. Meg knew that deep down. And, whether or not he had wanted it, still that love had existed. Her very brief marriage with him had for Meg been the real thing.

And, as Rosa had pointed out, they *were* still married.

It was getting cool, so Meg went inside and read the itinerary Rosa had handed her. Then she looked up the prison he was being held at and could not believe that he was even there, let alone that on Thursday she might be too.

Would be.

Meg slid the ring back on her finger.

A difficult decision, but somehow easily made. Yes, Rosa was right. In legal terms he was still her husband.

But it wasn't in legal terms only that she made her choice. There was a part of herself that she must soon sort out, must work out how to get over, but for now at least, in every sense, Niklas was still her husband.

Though her hotel and flights had been arranged, any problems had to be dealt with by the travel agent, Rosa had told her. Meg must not, under any circumstance, make contact with them. She must not be linked to them in any way—not just to protect them, or even Niklas, they had warned her, but to protect herself.

And she registered the danger but tried not to dwell on it, just tried to deal with a life that had changed all over again.

There was another row with her parents—a huge one this time. They had no comprehension as to why their usually sensible daughter might suddenly up and take off to Brazil.

'Brazil!' Her mother had just gaped. 'Why the hell do you want to go to Brazil?'

They didn't come to the airport to say good-bye. Still, there was one teeny positive to the whole situation: Meg barely noticed the plane taking off. Her thoughts were too taken up with the fact that she was on her way to see Niklas.

And she barely noticed it a second time, when she transferred at Santiago and knew she was on the last leg of her journey to see him. Shortly after take-off the stewards stood, and after a little while she was offered a drink.

'Tonic water...' Meg said, and then changed her mind and added gin.

'Off on holiday?'

She turned to her friendly fellow passenger, an elderly lady who had cousins in São Paulo, she told Meg.

'Yes...' Meg said. 'Sort of.'

'Visiting family?'

'My husband.' How strange it felt to say it, but she was, after all, wearing his ring, and her documents were in her bag, and she might have to say the same thing at Customs, so maybe she'd better start practising.

'Brazil first and then three weeks in Hawaii…'

'Lovely.' The old lady smiled and Meg returned it. Just as Niklas had that first day, she wished her neighbour would just keep quiet.

She could hardly tell her the real purpose for her visit!

Instead she ordered another gin.

It didn't help.

She cried as they descended over São Paulo— she had never seen anything like it. Stretched below her was a sea of city, endless miles of buildings and skyscrapers. The population of this city alone was almost equivalent to the entire population of Australia, and never had Meg felt more small and lost.

The final approach was terrifying—more so because of all he had told her about it, more so now that she could see just how closely the cars and the planes and the city co-existed, more so because she was actually here.

Bizarrely, her eyes searched for him after she'd cleared Customs—a stupid flare of hope that this was a strange joke, that he was testing her, that he might be waiting with flowers and a kiss. Perhaps she might once more feel the thorns press into her skin as he teased her about the lengths she'd go to for just a couple of hours with him.

It wasn't a joke, though. It wasn't a game. There was no one here to greet her.

Meg exited the airport and tried to hire a taxi, but she had never seen a taxi queue like this one. She was exhausted and overwhelmed as once again Niklas pushed her out of her comfort zone.

The driver's music was loud, his windows were down, and he drove her through darkening streets into Jardins. Everything was loud there too. The city pulsed with life. There were food stalls on the streets—unfamiliar scents came in through the windows of the car whenever they stopped at traffic lights—and it was more city than she could deal with. Which made sense, Meg thought with a pale smile. After all it was the city Niklas was from.

All Meg wanted to do was to get to her room.

Dishevelled, confused, *tired*, after they pulled up at a very tall hotel Meg paid the taxi driver. The second she stepped inside she knew she was back in his world.

Modern, cosmopolitan, with staff exquisite and beautiful.

It was a relief to get to her room and look out of the window at the bewildering streets below, to fathom that she was actually here—that tomorrow she would be taking another taxi to visit Niklas in prison.

Meg scanned the confusing horizon, wondered as to his direction, wondered if he had any inkling at all that she was even here.

Wondered all night how she could stand to face him tomorrow.

'Hi, Mum…' She rang not because they had insisted she did—they were hardly talking, after all—she rang because, despite their problems, Meg loved her parents and wanted the sound of normality tonight.

'How's Brazil?' Her mother's voice was terse, but at least she spoke.

'Amazing,' Meg said. 'Though I haven't seen much of it…'

'Have you booked any trips?'

'Not yet,' Meg said, and was quiet for a moment. She didn't like lying, especially to her parents, but she found herself doing it at every turn. Tomorrow she would be ringing her parents again to tell them that she had changed her mind about Brazil and was going to spend the rest of her vacation in Hawaii—how would they react to that?

More than anything Meg just wanted tomorrow over with, so that she could lie on a beach and hopefully heal once and for all. She hadn't dared risk putting her divorce application in her luggage in case it caused questions at Customs, but the second she landed home it would be posted.

Her heart couldn't take any more of him.

'How's Dad?'

'Worried,' her mum said, and Meg felt her heart sink—because she hated that they were worried about her. 'It's going to cost an arm and a leg to hire a new lawyer...'

Meg knew her mum didn't mean to hurt her, but unintentionally she had. The business was always the biggest thing on their minds.

'I've told you that I'll work for a couple of months when I get back. You don't have to rush into anything. And you don't need a full-time lawyer; you can contract out. We'll go through it all properly when I get back.'

'You *are* coming back?'

And Meg gave a small unseen smile, because maybe it wasn't just about the business. As difficult as they could be at times, they did want what they thought was best for her, and they did love her—that much Meg knew.

'Of course I am. I'm just taking a few weeks to sort out my head—I'll be back before you know it.'

It was impossible to sleep. She was dreading tomorrow and seeing him again, dreading the impact of seeing him face to face. It was emotionally draining just thinking about him, let alone seeing him.

Let alone having sex with him.

If Meg slept, she didn't sleep much, and she was up long before her alarm call. She ordered breakfast, but her stomach was doing somersaults and she could hardly manage to hold down a small piece of bread and grilled cheese.

The coffee she was more grateful for.

Had she not loved him, she doubted she could do this.

But had she not loved him she would not have

married him in the first place and wouldn't be in this mess.

Except she remembered his cruel words from that morning long ago and knew that love had no place in this.

She gave up on breakfast and lay in the bath, tried to prepare herself for what lay ahead, but had no idea how. As she picked up a razor and shaved her legs she did not know if her actions were for his pleasure or for her pride. It was the same with the body oil she rubbed in. She wore simple flesh-coloured underwear and an olive green shift dress with flat leather sandals. Her hand was shaking too much to bother with make-up so she gave in.

Rosa had given her the name of a good car company to use, rather than getting a taxi, and the desk rang to tell her that her driver was here. As she left the room she glanced around and wondered how she would feel when she returned. This time tomorrow she would be on a plane on her way to Hawaii. This time tomor-row it would be done—for despite what Rosa had said she would not be returning to him.

Once was enough.

Twice might kill her.

So she looked at her room and tried not to think too much about what had to happen be-fore she returned.

They drove through the most diverse of cities, passed the Court of Justice, where in two weeks Niklas would be, and in daylight Meg saw more of this stunning city. There was beauty and wealth, and such poverty too. She thought of Niklas growing up on the streets, and of how much he had made of himself only to fall. She didn't know enough to believe in his innocence. She might be a fool for love, but she wasn't a blind fool. Still, he deserved a fair trial.

Meg had never known such fear in her life as they approached the jail. The sight of the watch-tower, the sounds when she entered, the shame of the examination… Her papers were examined and her photograph taken and she was told her rights—or rather her husband's rights. She could return in three weeks; she could ring him once a week at a designated time and speak for ten minutes. And although Meg took the paper with the telephone number on it, she knew that she would never use it.

Then a female guard examined her for contraband and Meg closed her eyes, thinking she would spit at her if she ever faced Rosa again, before being allowed to pull her knickers back up. Maybe she did need to get over herself, but as she was led through to an area where two guards chatted she heard the Dos Santos name said a few times, and even if Meg didn't understand precisely what they were saying she got their lewd drift. As she stood waiting for Niklas to arrive Meg knew that, yes, she might have to get over herself—but right about now she was completely over *him*.

CHAPTER EIGHT

THE SLOT ON the door opened and lunch was delivered. Niklas ate beans and rice. It was tepid and bland and there were no herbs to pick out, but he was hungry and cleared his plate in silence.

His cellmate did the same.

It was how they both survived.

He refused to let the constant noise and shouts from other inmates rile him. He made no comment or complaint about the bland food and the filth. From the first day he had arrived here, apart from the odd necessary word, he had been silent, had conformed to the system though some of the guards had tried to goad him.

As he had entered the jail they had told him of the cellmate they had for him, of the beatings he could expect. They'd told the rich boy just how bad things would be in there for him as he'd removed his suit and shoes and then his watch and jewellry before they searched him and then hosed him.

Niklas had said nothing.

He had been hosed many times before.

There was no mirror to look in, so after his hair was shaved he'd just run a hand over his head. He wore the rough denim without real thought. He had worn harsher clothes and been filthier and hungrier than this on many occasion.

Niklas was streetwise. He had grown up in the toughest place and survived it. He had come from nothing and he'd returned to nothing— as he had always silently feared that he would. This anonymous, brutal world was one that he belonged in, and the one he truly deserved. Perhaps this was actually his home, Niklas had realised—not ten thousand feet in the air, swigging champagne as caviar popped in his mouth; not considering a home in the mountains and a family to take care of. He had been a fool to glimpse it, a fool to let down his guard, for those things were not his to know.

Assets frozen, friends and colleagues doubting him… The eventual snap of cuffs on his wrists had provided temporary relief as Niklas went back to the harsh world he had known one day would reclaim him. He'd returned to another system and navigated it seemingly with ease. But the temporary relief had soon faded and a sense of injustice had started to creep in. His head felt as if it would explode at times, and his body was so wired that he was sure he could rip the bars from the cell window with his bare hands or catch bullets with his teeth— but then, as he had long ago taught himself to, he simply turned those thoughts off.

Not for a second did he show his anger, and rarely did he speak.

His cellmate was one the most feared men in the prison. He ran the place and had contacts both inside and out. The guards had thought it would be like two bulls put in the same paddock. The motto of São Paulo was *I am not led. I lead.* So they had put the rich boy who led the business world in with the man who led the inmates and had waited for sobs from Dos Santos. But Niklas had held Fernando's eyes and nodded when he had been placed in his cell. He had said good evening and got no answer, and from that point on Niklas had said nothing more to him. He had ignored his cellmate—as suited Fernando, as suited him—and over the months the tension had dissipated. The silence between the two inmates was now amicable; both men respected the other's privacy, in a friendship of no words.

Niklas finished his lunch. He would exercise soon.

They had not been let out to the yard in over

a week, so in a moment he would use the floor to exercise. He paced himself, sticking to routines to hold onto his mind. For while he slotted in with the system, while he followed the prison rules, more and more he was starting to reject them. Inside a slow anger had long been building and it was one that must not explode, because he wanted to be here when his trial date was set—did not want solitary till then.

He lay on his bunk and tried not to build up too much hope that he might be bailed in a fortnight, when he appeared for the pre-trial hearing. Miguel had told him that he thought bail was unlikely—there were too many high-profile people involved who did not want him to have freedom.

'But there is no one involved,' Niklas had pointed out at their last meeting. 'Because I did not do anything. That is what you are supposed to prove.'

'And we will,' Miguel said.

'Where's Rosa?' Niklas had asked to see Rosa at this visit. He liked her straight talking, wanted to hear her take on things, but yet again it was Miguel who had come to meet with him.

'She...' Miguel looked uncomfortable. 'She wants to see you,' he said. 'I asked her to come in, but...'

'But what?'

'Silvio,' Miguel said. 'He does not want her in here with you.'

And Niklas got that.

Rosa's husband, Silvio, had complained about Rosa working for him. Niklas and Rosa had once been an item for a few weeks, just before she had met Silvio, and though there was nothing between them now, her working for Niklas still caused a few problems.

As he lay there replaying conversations, because that was all he was able to do in this place, Niklas conceded that Silvio was right not to want Rosa to visit him here.

Nothing would happen between them, but it was not just Rosa's sharp insight he wanted. The place stank of testosterone, of confined angry male, and Rosa was open enough to understand that his eyes would roam. She would let them, and he knew that she would dress well for him.

He tried not to think of Meg—did not want even an image of her in this place—but of course it was impossible not to think of her.

As his mind started to drift he turned those thoughts off and hauled them back to his pre-trial hearing. His frustration at the lack of progress was building—his frustration at everything was nearing breaking point.

He climbed down from his bunk and started doing sit-ups, counting in his head. And then he changed to push-ups, and for those he did not bother to count. He would just work till his body ached. But anger was still building. He wanted to be on the outside—not just for freedom but because there he could control things, and he could control nothing here except his small routines. So he kept on doing his sit-ups and as a guard came to the door Niklas carried on, ignoring the jeering, just kept on with his workout.

'Lucky man, Dos Santos.'

He did not miss a beat, just continued his exercise.

'Who did you pay?'

Still Niklas did not answer.

'You have a beautiful wife.'

Only then did he pause, just for a second, mid-push-up, before carrying on. The guard didn't know what he was talking about. No one knew of Meg—they were winding him up, messing with his head, and he chose not to respond.

'She's here waiting to see you.'

And then the slot in the door opened and he was told to get up. There was no choice now but to do as he was told. So Niklas stood, met Fernando's eyes for just a second, which was rare. The change in routine was notable for both of them.

Niklas put his hands through the slot and handcuffs were applied, then he pulled his cuffed wrists back as the cell door was opened. He walked along the corridor and down metal steps, heard the jeers and taunts and crude re-marks as he walked past. There were a couple of shoves from the guard but Niklas did not react, just kept on walking while trying to work things out.

Miguel must have arranged a hooker, finally pulled a few strings.

Thank God.

Maybe now his mind would hold till the trial date.

Not that he showed any emotion as they walked. He'd learnt that many years ago.

Show weakness and you lose—he'd learnt that at eight.

He had walked through the new orphanage

he'd been sent to—he had been on his third orphanage by then—and this one was by far the worst. Still, there was good news, he had been told—his new family were waiting to meet him. A beautiful family, the worker had told him. They were rich, well fed and well dressed and had everything they wanted in the world except children. More than anything they wanted a son and had chosen Niklas.

His heart had leapt in hope. He'd hated the orphanage, a rough home for boys where the staff were often cruel, and he had been grinning and excited as the door had been pushed open and he had prepared himself to meet his new family.

How the workers waiting for him in there had laughed at his tears—how they had jeered him, enjoying their little joke long into the night. How could he have been so bold as to think that a family might want him?

It was the very last time that Niklas had cried.

His last display of true emotion.

Now he kept it all inside.

He would not give the prison guards the same pleasure. Whatever their plan, he would not give them the satisfaction of reading his face.

But then he saw her.

It had not properly entered his head that it might actually be Meg.

He had not allowed it to.

She did not belong in here. That was his first thought as he saw her dressed in a linin shift dress. Her hair burned gold and copper, the colour of the sun at night through his cell window, and then he saw the anxiety in her eyes turn to horror as she took in the shaved head and the rough clothing. A lash of shame tore through him that he should be seen by her like this, and his expression slipped for just a second. He stared ahead as his cuffs were removed, and though he remained silent his mind raced. To the left was Andros, the guard he trusted the least, and he thought again how Meg did not belong here. He wanted to know who the hell had arranged this, who had approved this visit, for even though he was confined and locked up he still had a system in place, and he had told Miguel that everything was to be run by him.

He could feel Andros watching as she walked towards him, heard the fear and anxiety in her voice as she spoke.

'I've missed you so much.'

She was playing a part. Niklas got that. But as her lips met his cheek it did not matter. Her touch was the first reprieve for his senses in months. Her skin on his cheek was so soft that the contact actually shocked him. He wanted to know the hows and whys of her visit here, wanted to know exactly what was going on, yet his first instinct was not to kiss her, but to protect her—and that meant that he too must play a part, for Andros was watching.

It was a kiss for others, and his mind tried to

keep it at that—except her breath tasted of the outside and he drank her in. The feel of her in his arms allowed temporary escape and it was Meg who pulled back.

Meg stood with her cheeks burning red, tears of shame and hurt and anger in her eyes, and her lips pressed closed as one guard said something that made the other laugh. Then a door opened and they walked into a small, simply furnished room. The guard shouted something to them, and whatever language you spoke it was crude, before closing the door behind them. Meg stood and then realised that she couldn't stand for very much longer, so she sat on a chair for a moment, honestly shaken.

It wasn't just shock at the sight of him—seeing Niklas with his hair cropped almost as short as the dark stubble on his chin, dressed in rough prison denim. Even like this he was still the most beautiful man she had ever seen. It was not just the shock that she had again tasted his mouth, felt his skin against hers, relighting all those memories from their one night together. It was everything: the whole journey here, the poverty in the streets she had driven through, the sight of the prison as she had approached, the watchtower and the guns on the guards and the shame of the strip-search. Surely all of those things had severed any feelings she had for him?

But, no, for then she'd had to deal with the impact of seeing him again, of tasting him. For a moment she just sat there and wondered how, after all she had been through, she could still hear her heart hammer in relief to be back at his side. She wanted to be over him—had to be for sanity's sake—so she tried not to look at him, just drank from the glass of water he offered her.

He stood and watched her and saw her shock, saw what just a little while in this place had done to her, and thought again how she did not belong here.

'Why?' He knelt down beside her and spoke in a rough whisper. 'Why would you come here?'

She didn't answer him—Meg couldn't open her mouth to speak.

'Why?' he demanded, and then she looked at him and he was reminded of the last time he had seen her. Because even with the absence of her bared teeth he could feel her anger, could see her green eyes flash with suppressed rage and hear the spit of her words when finally she answered him.

'You're *entitled* to me, apparently.'

Niklas remembered the first time he had met her. She had been anxious, but happy, and he knew that it was he who had reduced her to this. He could see the pain and the disgust in her eyes as she looked at the man she had married, as she saw the nothing he really was.

And he did not want her charity.

'Thanks, but no thanks.'

He moved to the door, preparing to call for

the guards. He might regret it later, but he did not want a minute more in this room.

As he moved to go he heard her voice.

'Niklas.' She halted him. This was not about what had happened between them, not about scoring points, she was here for one reason only. 'Your people told me...' He turned to face her. 'I'm to tell you...'

He silenced her by pressing his finger to his lips and nodded to the door. He trusted no one—never had in his life, and wasn't about to start in here. But then he closed his eyes for a second, for that was wrong. Because for a while he had trusted *her*, and did still. He came over to her, knelt down again and moved his head to her mouth, so she could quietly tell him the little she knew.

'Miguel is working against you. You are to ask for a change of representation at your trial...'

His head pulled back and she watched as he took in the news. Quietly she told him the little she knew. His face was grey and his eyes shone black. He swallowed as if tasting bile and she heard his rapid angry breathing. His whisper was harsh when it came.

'*No.*'

It had to be a lie, because if his own lawyer was working against him he was here for life.

She *had* to be lying.

'How?' he demanded. 'Why?'

'I don't know anything more than that,' Meg said. 'It's all I've been told.'

'When?' he insisted, his voice an angry whisper. 'When were you told?'

And she told him about the visit—how on Monday morning Rosa and her colleagues had arrived at her place of work. He thought of her momentarily in Sydney, getting on with her life without him, and now here she was in Brazil.

'They should never have sent you…' He was livid. 'It's too dangerous…'

'It's fine…'

It was so *not* fine.

'Niklas…' She told him *all* they had told her—that they had to have sex, about the bed and the bin, and that the guards could not know she was here for any other reason.

He saw her face burn in shame, and she saw his disgust at what he had put her through.

'It's fine, Niklas,' she whispered. 'I know what I'm doing…' She could feel his fury; it was there in the room with them.

'You should not be here.'

'It's my decision.'

'Then it's the wrong one.'

'I'm very good at making those around you, it would seem. Anyway,' she whispered harshly, 'you don't have to worry—you're paying me well…'

'How much?'

She told him.

And he knew then the gravity of his situation, understood just how serious this was—because he had no money any more. Everything had been frozen. He thought of his legal team paying her with money of their own and it tempered the bitterness that sometimes consumed him a little. Then he looked at the woman he might even have loved and tasted bitterness one again, for he hated what the world had done to him.

'So you're not here out of the goodness of your heart?'

'You've already had that part,' Meg said. 'So can we just get it over with?'

She looked over to the bed and he saw the swallowing in her throat, knew that she was drenched in fear. He looked to the door again, knowing there was a guard outside, one he did not trust, who must never get so much as a hint as to the real reason she was here.

Paid to be here, Niklas reminded himself.

He trusted no one again.

He stood and ripped the sheet from the bed, and she sat there as he twisted it in his hands before throwing it back. She heard his anger as he took the bedhead in angry hands and rocked the bed against the wall. He felt his anger building as he slammed the bed faster and faster. He had never paid for sex in his life. Yes, he'd have been grateful for a hooker, but he'd never taken Meg as one and his head was pounding as the bed hit the wall again and again. He did not know who to believe any more, and as the bed slammed faster he shouted out.

Meg sobbed as he shouted, but it did nothing to dissipate the fury still building, and then he picked up the condoms by the bedside and went to the small wash area and got to work to make sure evidence of their coupling was in place. Meg sat there, listening and crying. She understood his anger but she did not understand her own self, for even here, amidst this filth and shame, she wanted him. So badly she wanted to be with the man she had so sorely missed. Not just the sex, but the comfort he somehow gave.

'Niklas…' She walked into the washroom and ignored him when he told her, less than politely, to go away. His back was to her. She moved to his side and saw his fury, saw his hand working fast. He repeated his demand for her to leave him, and when it was clear that she didn't understand just how much he meant the words he told her in French and then Spanish.

'How many ways do you need to hear it…?'

How deep was his shame to be seen like this, to be reduced to this? His back had been to Meg, for he could not face her, yet she'd slipped into the space between him and the wall and her mouth was on his. One of her hands joined his now.

'Leave me.'

'No.' She stroked him too.

'Leave me,' he said as her other hand slipped off her panties.

'No.'

And she put her hands around his neck and

pressed herself against him, tried to kiss him. He spat her out.

'You don't know the fire you are playing with.'

'I want to, though.'

She wanted every piece of him—wanted a little more of what she could never fully have. Because a man like Niklas could only ever be on loan to her. She had flown to him not because she had to, not for the money, and not for the morality of doing the right thing by her husband. Purely because of him, and not once did his anger scare her.

Not once, as rough hands pulled her dress up, did she fear him.

He lifted her up and onto him and positioned her, pulling her roughly down to him. The most basic sex was their only release and she wrapped her legs tight around him, locked her arms around his neck. His kiss was violent now, and she felt the clash of their teeth and tongues and the rapid angry stabs of him. The rough feel of denim on her thighs was nothing compared to the roughness deep inside, and her back was hard against the wall. Meg could feel his anger, it blasted deep inside her, and it let Meg be angry too—angry at so many things: that she was here, that she still wanted him, even that this man still moved her so.

Her moans and shouts that he blocked with his mouth shocked Meg even more—scared her, almost—but she was not scared of him as he pulled her down on him, as she felt the bruise of his fingers in her hips. She could feel her orgasm building rapidly, as if she had waited eleven months just to come to him, as if her body had been waiting for him to set it free.

There was a flash of confusion for Niklas too, for her cries and the grip of intimate muscles, the arch of her back and the spasm of her thighs, could never be faked. He had thought this was charity, a paid act at best, a sympathy screw at worst, but she was craving him again, the way she once had, and as he shot into her he remembered all the good again—the way they had been. He never cried, but he was as close to it now as he had ever been. They were both drenched in brief release and escape and his kisses turned softer now, to bring her back to him. Then he heard the drizzle of the tap and his eyes opened to his surroundings, to the reality they faced. There were no more kisses to be had and he lifted her off.

Stood her down.

But she would not lose him to his pride and she carried on kissing him, opened his shirt and put her palms to his chest. He felt as if her hands seared him, for there had been no contact, no touch of another on his skin for many months, and he loathed the exposure, the prying of her hands. It was just sex he wanted, not her, but her hands were still moving, exploring the defined muscles. Her fingers were a pleasure and he did not want her to be here—yet he wanted her for every second that they had.

There would be hours later for thinking, for working out what to do about Miguel. For now he wanted every minute he had left with her.

He took her to the bed and undressed her, took his clothes off too, and she looked at all the changes to his body. He was thinner, but more muscled, and his face wasn't the one she had turned to on the plane—it was closed and angry, and yet she had felt his pain back there, felt him slip into affection, and for a small moment had glimpsed the man she had once met.

'Is that why you ended things?' She looked over to him as he joined her on the bed, but he just lay and looked up at the ceiling. 'Did you find out the trouble you were in?'

'I didn't know then.' It would be easier for her if he lied.

'So what happened that morning to change things?'

'I spoke to my people at work, realised how much I had on…'

'I don't believe you.'

'Believe in your fairytale if you want.' Niklas shrugged.

'Are you going to tell me to grow up again?' she asked. 'Because I grew up a long time ago—long before you met me. I've realised that I wasn't being weak staying in my job—I simply won't ride roughshod over the people I care about. And I don't believe that you would either and,' she finished, 'I *do* believe that you cared about me.'

'Believe what you want to.'

'I will,' Meg said. 'And I care about you.'

'It makes no difference to me.'

She had been paid plenty to be here with him so he should turn and start things. She had told him what she had came to say and the clock was counting down. He should use every minute wisely. They should not bother with talking—there were more basic things to be getting on with. Except this was Meg, and she didn't know how to separate the two.

'How are you dealing with being in here? How—?' she started, but he soon interrupted.

'I was right the first time.' He turned to look at her face—the face he had first seen on a plane. 'You talk too much. And I don't want to talk about me.' But before he moved to kiss her he allowed himself the luxury of just one question. 'Are you still working for your parents?'

'I resigned…' Meg said. 'I'm trying to choose my course at the moment…'

'Good,' Niklas said. He should push her hand down to where he was hardening again, but first there was something else he wanted to know. 'Are you okay?'

'Of course.'

'Are you happy?'

'Working on it.'

'Do your parents know you are here?'

'They know that I am in Brazil…' he saw tears pool in her eyes '…they don't know I have a husband that I'm visiting in prison.'

'You need to get away from here,' Niklas said. 'As soon as this visit is over.'

'I fly to Hawaii tomorrow.'

'Okay.' Tomorrow should be okay, he told himself, but he wasn't sure. 'Maybe change it to tonight…'

'I fly out at six a.m.'

He saw her grimace at the thought, remembered the first time they had met and the conversation they had had.

'How was your landing?' And for the first time he smiled. He didn't care how much they'd paid her, that she'd flown into Congonhas was enough for him to know that this had nothing to do with money.

'It wasn't so bad…' she attempted, and then told him the truth. 'I was petrified. I thought I was going to throw up. Although,' she added, 'that might have been the gin!'

He laughed, and so did she. He hadn't laughed for almost a year, but this afternoon he did. She kicked him and they fought for a bit—a nice fight, a friendly fight—and he took her back to when they'd been lovers so easily, far, far too easily. But, given this was the last time she would be here, she let him. No one could kiss like he did. It was quite simply perfect, and the feel of him hard in her hands was perfect too.

This time he would be gentle, Niklas decided, worried that he had been too rough before. He didn't just kiss her mouth, he kissed her everywhere—her hair and her ears and down to her neck, breathing in her scent. He kissed down to her waist and then further, to where he wanted to be. He had been too rough, for she was hot and swollen, but Meg lay there and felt his soft kiss and was lost to it.

When he couldn't hold on any more he reached

for the condom that was a requirement in here. Her hands reached for it too, and he let her put it on, but before she did she kissed him there, and he closed his eyes as she did so. Two hours could never be enough for all they wanted to do. She slid it on. He should roll her over and take her, but he let her climb on top of him, because if he looked up to her hair and her body for a little while he could forget where he was.

And she looked down as she moved on him and knew exactly why she was here. She loved him. Still. Her real fear at coming here had nothing to do with the flight or the prison or the danger, it was *him*—because she'd known all along that this was the only way she would ever be over him.

She should be grilling him about his involvement in the charges, insisting she find out, or just lying on her back martyred as he took her, ready to get the hell out once he'd finished. Instead she'd told him she cared about him. Instead she was riding him, and his hands were busy elsewhere, roaming her body. He was watching her. She was moaning, and he told her to hush, for he would not give the guards the turn-on of the sounds that she made. He put his hand over her mouth and she licked it, bit it, and he pushed his fingers into her mouth. He was coming, and so was she, and when the moment finally came she folded on top of him, buried his face with her hair, and he felt the silent scream inside her as she clutched him tightly over and over till it ended.

That was when she told him she loved him.

'You don't know me,' he said.

'I want to, though.'

'Divorce me,' he said, still inside her, and pulled her close. 'Send the papers to Rosa and I'll sign them.'

'I don't want to.'

'You do.'

She didn't.

'I can see you again in three weeks…' She was drunk on him. 'I can come to the trial.'

'You are to *leave*!'

'I can ring you on Wednesday each week…'

He was scared now as to what he'd unleashed. Scared not of her passion, but that she might stay.

'No.'

'I can. I'm allowed one phone call a week.'

He looked up at her and all he knew was that she was not coming back here. With his own lawyer working against him he was probably done. Here was where he would always be and he would not do this to her. Even with new lawyers, trials took for ever in Brazil. Even with the best legal team he would be here for years at best. He lifted her off him and swore in three languages when he saw the condom was shredded. 'Get the morning-after pill and when I speak with my new lawyers I will have them file for divorce…'

'No...'

'You are to go to Hawaii.'

'Niklas—'

The guards were knocking at the door. Their time was up. He stood and threw her clothes at her, telling her to dress quickly for he did not want them getting one single glimpse of her. She continued to argue with him as he picked up her bra and clipped it on her, before lifting each leg into her panties, followed by her dress, and even as he zipped it up still she argued.

'We're finished,' he told her.

And he wasted time telling her that they *had* to be over when he should have told her how dangerous this was, just how little he knew about what was going on, and that he was scared for her life. But the guards were here now and he could not say.

He gave her a brief kiss, his eyes urging her. 'Have a safe flight.'

CHAPTER NINE

SHE DIDN'T WANT to lie on a beach in Hawaii.

There could be no healing from him.

She wanted to be close to him, wanted to be there for his trial hearing at least. She hoped for a miracle.

He would not want her there. Meg knew that.

But he was her husband, and she could at least be here in the city for him. Could watch it on the news, could be close even if he didn't know it.

And then she could visit him again before she left. She did not want a divorce from him now, and she wanted one more visit to argue her case.

She was probably going insane, Meg realised as she cancelled Hawaii and stayed on in Brazil, but that was how he made her feel.

She ventured out onto the busy streets and

toured the amazing city. The sights, the smells, the food, the noise—there was everything to meet her moods.

And without Niklas she might never have seen any of this—might never have visited the Pinacoteca, a stunning art museum, nor seen the sculptured garden beside it.

At first Meg did guided tours with lots of other tourists around her, but gradually she tuned in to the energy of the place, to the smiles and the thumbs-up from the locals and ventured out more alone. She was glad to be here— glad for everything she got to see, to hear, to feel. Every little thing. She could have lived her whole life and never tasted *pamonah*, and there were vendors selling them everywhere—from the streets, from cars, ringing triangles to alert they were here. The first time Meg had bought one and had sunk her teeth into the new taste of mashed and boiled corn she had been unable to finish it. But the next day she had been back, drawn by the strange sweet taste—inadvertently she'd bought savoury, and found that was the one she liked best.

There were so many things to learn.

So badly she wanted to visit the mountains, to take a trip to the rainforests Niklas had told her about, yet it felt too painful to visit the mountains without him.

She didn't dare ring him that first week. Instead when six p.m. on Wednesday neared she sat in a restaurant the concierge had told her was famed for its seafood and ordered *feijoada*. Maybe it wasn't the same restaurant Niklas had told her about, but she felt as if angels were feeding her soul and that she was right to be there.

As the days passed she fell more and more in love with the city—the contrasts of it, the feel of it and the sound of it. The people were the most beautiful and elegant she had seen, yet the poverty was confrontational. It was a world that changed at every turn and she loved the anonymity of being somewhere so huge, loved being lost in it, and for two weeks she was.

As instructed, she did not contact Rosa. The only people she spoke to were her parents, and she gave Niklas no indication that she was there until the night before his trial date.

His face was on the TV screen, a reporter was already outside the court, and Meg had worked out that *amanhã* meant tomorrow. Until *amanhã* she simply could not wait. She just had to hear his voice. She had fallen in love with a man who was in prison and she should be signing paperwork, should be happily divorced, should be grateful for the chance to resume her life—but instead she sat in her hotel room, staring at the phone…

Confused was all she was without him. The passion and love she felt for him only made real sense when he was near her and she had an overwhelming desire to talk to him. She counted down the moments until she could make that call.

* * *

He knew that she would call.

Niklas could feel it.

Andros came and got him from his cell and he sat by the phone at the allotted time. The need for her to be safe overrode any desire to hear her voice.

His teeth gritted when he heard the phone ring, and he wondered if he should let it remain unanswered, but he needed her to get the message—to get out of his life and leave him the hell alone.

And then he heard her voice and realised just how much he craved it, closed his eyes in unexpected relief just to hear the sound of her.

'I told you not to ring.'

'I just wanted to wish you good luck for tomorrow.'

'It is just to arrange a trial date...' He did not trust the phones. He did not trust himself. For now he wanted her to visit him again. He wanted her living in a house in the mountains right behind the prison and wanted her to ring him every Wednesday, to come in to see him every three weeks. What scared him the most was that she might do it. 'You did not need to ring for that. It will all be over in ten minutes.'

She understood the need to be careful. 'Even so, I hope they give you a date soon.'

'What are you doing now?'

'Talking to you.'

'Is everything okay?'

She knew what he was referring to—had seen his face when he'd removed the condom.

'It's fine.'

'Did you go to a *pharmacia*?'

He closed his eyes when she didn't answer, thought again of her in a home in the mountains, but this time he pictured her with his baby at her side and selfish hope glimmered.

'How's Hawaii?'

He heard her pause, heard that her voice was

a little too high as she answered him. 'You know…' She attempted. 'Nice.'

'I *don't* know,' Niklas said, and it was not about what he wanted, it was not about him, it was about keeping her safe. His words were harsh now. 'I've never been and I want a postcard,' he said. 'I want you, *tonight*, to write me a postcard from Hawaii.'

He was telling her what to do and she knew it.

'Niklas,' she attempted, 'I still have some holidays left. I thought maybe next week…'

'You want to be paid again?'

'Niklas, please—' She hated that he'd mentioned money. 'I just want to see you.'

'You've already earned your keep…go spend your money on holiday.'

'Niklas…I know you don't mean that.'

'*What* do you know?' His voice was black. 'We were married for one day; we screwed an awful lot. You know nothing about me.'

'I know that you care. I know when you saw me—'

'Care?' he sneered down the phone. 'The only way I can get sex in here is if they bring in my wife—that's it. I am sick of conversations, and you seem to want just as many of those as you give of the other.'

'Niklas, please…'

But he would not let her speak. He had to get her away from here. Did she not get that she could be in danger? He had no idea what was happening on the outside, had no idea what was going on, and he wanted her safely away—had to make sure she was safe.

So again he drowned her with words.

'Meg, if you want to come back and suck me, then do. But just so long as you know you mean nothing to me.'

He slammed down the phone—not in fury but in fear. He put his hands through the door and felt the cool of the cuffs. His mind was racing.

Since her visit, since getting the information that Miguel was working against him, his mind had been spinning, trying to work out what the hell was going on, trying to figure things out. But now he had a head full of *her*, and he had more to be concerned with than that she was still here in Brazil.

He needed to speak with Rosa—had to work out what the hell was going on.

As he was walked back to his cell his face was expressionless, but his mind was pounding like a jackhammer and he cursed under his breath in Portuguese as Andros made some reference to his wife, about his nice little family, and asked how scum from the streets had managed that. Then Andros pushed him up the stairs and Niklas cursed again, but in French this time.

'Watch it, Dos Santos...' Andros told him, sensing his prisoner's rising anger and slamming him up against the wall.

The move was not meant to overpower him,

Niklas realised, simply to provoke him, because Dos Santos was an orphan's name. Niklas went to swear again, in Spanish, but his brain was working quickly, far more quickly than his mouth, and in that second he knew what was happening.

Dos Santos meant something different in Spanish.

And it was a Spanish nun who had named him.

Dos Santos in Spanish meant two saints.

He had a twin.

In that very second it was as if a bomb had exploded in his brain and he worked it all out. He knew instantly how he had got to be here. Knew that his double was out there and had been working with Miguel against him. And with a lurch of fear that was violent to his soul he knew that Meg was in serious danger.

Niklas said nothing when Andros jeered again, just stood silent against the wall as Andros spoke filth about his wife. He stood still and refused to react as another guard came over. A decent guard this time, because there were plenty of them around.

'Trouble?' the guard asked.

'No trouble,' Niklas said, because he did not want to go to solitary tonight. He really needed to get to his cell.

He stood compliant as his cuffs were removed and went quietly into his cell. There he met the eyes of Fernando, and for the first time since his arrival he spoke with the other man.

'I need your help,' Niklas said, for he had worked out what was happening and urgent help was required. 'I need you to make contact on the outside.'

CHAPTER TEN

ANOTHER NIGHT CRYING over Niklas Dos Santos and Meg swore it would be the last.

Part of her could almost convince herself that he was just trying to get her to leave, that that was the reason behind his cruel words, but the more sensible part of Meg soon talked herself round. Her sensible side reminded her that this was a man she knew nothing about—a man who had caused her nothing but heartache and trouble since the day that they had met.

Hawaii sounded pretty good to Meg right now.

A week lying on the beach concentrating on nothing but how best to forget him.

It was well after lunchtime now, and Meg was *still* waiting for the travel agent to return her call. When she did, Meg would ask to be booked onto the earliest flight that could be arranged, and she packed her suitcase in preparation. Very deliberately she did not turn on the vast television to see how his trial was going, or to catch a glimpse of him on the news, because one glimpse of Niklas and she was lost to him—that much she knew.

She wanted her divorce now, wanted to be the hell away from him, would not waste even one more single minute on him.

But as she packed up her toiletries Meg threw tampons into her make-up bag and suddenly realised that it might be rather more complicated than that.

She looked at the unopened packet, an Australian brand because she hadn't bought any since she had arrived here, and tried to remember when she'd last had a period.

She tried to remember the days in Australia before her life had been changed so dramatically by the visit from Niklas's lawyers. No, she hadn't had her period for a while.

There should be the reassurance that they'd used condoms, but the last one hadn't held.

Could she be pregnant?

Would she tell him if she was?

Meg looked in the mirror and decided that, no, she could not deny him that. Even if his life was to be spent on the inside, he would have to know the truth, and it wasn't the kind of news she could reveal in a letter—maybe she would have to visit him again.

Maybe not.

A letter was probably more than he deserved.

But first she had to know for sure.

She was probably overreacting, Meg told herself as she headed out of her hotel room and to the elevators. Worrying too much, she tried to convince herself as she headed onto the street. With all that she'd been through these past weeks it was no wonder that her period was late.

The streets were busy, as always—the cars jammed together, horns blaring, and sirens blazing as police tried to thread their way through the impossible madness that was downtown São Paulo. She found a *pharmacia* and inside it was the same as the world over, with numerous pregnancy testing kits sitting on the shelves. Meg didn't need to speak the language to know she was making the right purchase.

What was different from Australia, though, was that instead of being pounced on by an assistant the second she entered the store, here Meg was pretty much ignored. Even when she tried to pay the pharmacist and his checkout assistants were all taking an impromptu break and watching the television, and Meg could feel mounting impatience. She really had to know now if she was pregnant. Had to make the decision of facing Niklas and telling him while she was still here.

Finally someone came over to serve her, still

talking to her colleagues, and Meg froze when she heard one of them shout the name Dos Santos. She felt sweat bead on her forehead as she paid, because despite herself—despite all this— she wanted to turn the television on, wanted to know how he was.

She almost ran back to the hotel, terrified of her feelings for him, that even a mention of his name could reduce her to this petrified state.

It was blissfully cool and quiet in her room— such a contrast to the chaos down below. She fought not to turn on the television, picked up the remote and hurled it, tried not to look where it landed. The light on the phone said she had a new message. She hoped it was the travel agent and played it back, but heard her mum's voice instead. Meg honestly didn't know how she could ever begin tell her parents all that had happened. She had always hoped she would never have to, but if this test proved positive…

She could feel the tears starting again but refused to give in to them—just bit them back and headed to the bathroom, put her purchase in its bag on the bench, ready to find out. Then there was a knock on the door and Meg assumed it was the cleaner. She didn't want her coming in now. She wanted privacy for this at least.

So she went to tell them. She didn't even look through the peephole, just opened the door, and what was left of the sensible part of her mind struggled to remain calm because standing at her door was Niklas. She froze for a moment, unable to respond to seeing him in such an ordinary setting. She wanted to sob at him, to rage at him, to ask him how on earth he was here— except she just stood there.

'It's okay…' He stepped in. 'I know it must be a shock to see me here.'

'I don't understand…'

'The judge understood,' he said. 'Didn't you see it all on the news?'

'I haven't been watching it.'

'That is good.' He gave her a smile. 'I get to tell you the good news myself.'

'I don't want to hear it.' She was so very angry with him, and now finally she could tell him. 'I haven't been watching it because I'm sick of this, Niklas. I'm sick of how you make me feel at times. I can't do this any more.'

'You're upset.'

'Do you blame me?' She looked at him. She could smell his cologne—the same cologne he had worn the day they had met. He was dressed in a stunning suit now, just as beautiful as the day they had met, just as cruel as the day he had ended things between them, but she wanted to know. 'You've been let off?'

'I've been bailed while they take some time to review new evidence.'

'Well, after the way you spoke to me last night I need some time for a review too,' Meg answered. She refused just to go back to loving him. He had hurt her too much. And she could not find out if she was pregnant while he was near. She needed to do that part alone.

'Come here...' He moved to pull her into his arms.

'Just leave.' It took everything she had to shake her head. 'Just go, Niklas. I'm doing as you told me. I'm going to Hawaii...'

'You're upset.'

'Why do you keep saying that? Of *course* I'm upset!' she flared. 'Did you think I wouldn't be? How the hell do you justify speaking to me like that?'

'Meg...'

He walked over and she did *not* want him to take her in his arms, did not want him to melt her all over again.

'I say stupid things at times. You know that...'

'Stupid things?' There were so many other ways she could describe his words. 'It was more than stupid, it was foul...' She would not be fobbed off. 'Why?' she demanded. 'Why did you speak to me like that?'

'I've said I'm sorry.'

'No, you haven't, and you're clearly not as sorry as I was to hear it.' She went to open the door, to tell him to get out of here, but he stopped her and wrapped his arms around her shoulders. Meg just stood there, tears rising, remembering the love they had made and all the ways he made her feel. But she could not go back there. 'Get out!' She pushed him off her. 'I mean it, Niklas...'

'Meg...' His mouth was on her cheek and she pulled her head away. His hands were in her hair but she brushed them off.

'Please,' she said, 'can you just leave me? I'll call you later. I'll—'

His phone rang then, and it annoyed her that he took the call. Yes, of course he was busy, she knew that, and maybe she should be flattered that he had come straight to her, but it annoyed her that in the middle of a row he could just stop and take a call. It made her even more angry, and she was tired of making excuses for him. She wanted him gone and she told him so when he ended his call.

'You are cross…' He smiled at her. 'You look beautiful when you are cross…'

He aimed his phone at her and she blinked at the flash. 'What the hell are you doing?'

'I've missed things like this. I want to capture everything…'

'I just you want you to leave.'

But he simply refused to listen. 'Let's go for a walk.'

'A walk?'

The last thing she wanted was a walk. She wanted him to leave. She looked at his lips and not even his beautiful mouth could silence her doubts now. She just wanted him gone.

'A walk to clear the air…' Niklas said.

'No.' She shook her head. 'I'm waiting for the travel agent to ring me back.'

'She'll call back if you're not here.' He

shrugged. 'Come,' he said. 'I want to taste the fresh air. I want to feel the rain...'

She looked out of the window. Yes, it was raining, and she realised that he wouldn't have felt the rain in a long time. She was relieved that he wasn't all over her, trying to kiss her back to confusion as he so often did, but she didn't feel she knew him at all.

'Meg, after all we have been through will you at least come for a walk with me?'

'You hurt me last night.'

'I apologise.' His black eyes met hers. 'Meg, I truly apologise. We can start again, without all this hanging over us...'

But she was stronger than she'd thought she could be.

She looked into his eyes and quite simply no longer wanted him—didn't want to get back on the rollercoaster ride beside him. It was then that she made a decision that was surprisingly easy; she looked at the man who had broken her heart and knew that he would break it all over again. She simply refused to let him.

It was over.

Whatever the pregnancy test told her, Meg knew it was far better that she find out well away from him. She would fly to Hawaii today, search for the clarity he so easily clouded and make better decisions alone.

'Come…' he said. 'I want to taste my freedom.'

Maybe it would be easier to tell him that they were finished while they were walking. Maybe it would prove easier out there. Because she knew his kisses made her weak. So she nodded and she went to get her jacket, to comb her hair.

'Don't worry about that…' he said. 'Your hair is fine…'

Niklas was right. Her hair really didn't matter right now—it was her heart Meg had to worry about. They rode down in the lift together and Meg looked at him more closely. She hated her swollen eyes. Even more she hated that she had let him cause them.

They headed out through the foyer and into the street and she felt the warm rain that was so regular here. His hand reached for her, but she pulled hers back, refusing to give this man any more chances. He'd already used his last one with his filthy words to her the previous night and now his pathetic attempt at an apology.

'I'm ending it, Niklas.' He kept on walking. 'I'm going to file for divorce.'

'We'll go to a bar and talk about it.'

'There's nothing to discuss.' Meg stopped—which wasn't the most sensible thing to do on such a busy street.

There were moans from a few pedestrians and he took her hand and they kept walking. She really was sure that she was making the right choice, because she did not know him, and he did not know her, and a walk would not clear the air. Only his kiss could possibly have given them a chance, because sex was the only thing they had going for them. Maybe she was mad for thinking it, but shouldn't that be the way a man celebrated his freedom? If he loved her, if he wanted her, wouldn't the first thing he wanted be taking her to bed, not out for a walk?

'There's a bar up here that I know,' Niklas said. 'It's not far—just a couple of blocks away…'

'I don't want to go to a bar…'

'The street is too noisy. Come on, we can talk properly there.'

'I don't want to talk.'

Meg was starting to panic now, and she didn't really know why. His hand was too tight on her wrist, and he was walking her faster, and she had the most appalling thought then that he hadn't been bailed at all. There was an urgency in the steps he was taking. She looked over to him and his head was down, and it dawned on Meg that maybe he had escaped from jail.

She recalled the screams of the police cars and bikes. They were screaming in the streets even louder now. She remembered too the pharmacy staff all huddled around the television, saying his name. Maybe it was because Niklas Dos Santos had escaped. Still he walked her ever faster.

'Niklas...'

She could hear the thud of music as they turned into a side street, could hear the clang of triangles and the smell of *pamonah*. There were so many people around; surely she was safe. She pulled her hand from his and stopped walking, but he turned and put a hand to her cheek. She shivered, but not with pleasure. There was something dark and menacing in his eyes. She was a fool to have got involved with this man, a fool to follow her heart, for look where it had led her—to a dingy side street in Brazil with a man she was now terrified of.

'Come,' he said. 'We will talk about where

our relationship is going later. Right now I want to celebrate my freedom and I want you to celebrate it with me.' His hand was tight on her arm. 'You wouldn't deny me that?'

'I do,' she said. 'And I want you to let me go.'

'Don't spoil this day for me, Meg—it's been a hell of a long year for both of us. Now we can drink *cachaca*, unwind, dance. Later we can talk, but first...'

He lowered his head to kiss her, but it was too late for that and she moved her head back from his, suddenly confused. Because Niklas didn't dance. It was one of the few things that she *did* know about him—or had that been just another of his lies? Suddenly she was scared, and with real reason now.

Meg turned to go but he pulled her roughly back and pushed her against the wall. Then he opened his jacket and she saw that he had a gun.

'Try to run and it will be the last thing you do...'

'Niklas…' she begged, and when Meg heard her own voice she heard the way she sounded when she pleaded for her life. She was trying to show him that she wasn't panicked, trying to reason with a man she absolutely didn't know, trying to get away. 'Why do you need me?' she said. 'If you've escaped…'

People were turning to look at them, maybe alerted by the panic in her voice even though she wasn't screaming. Or perhaps it was that if he had just escaped then his picture would be everywhere, being flashed over the news. Perhaps that was why he lowered his face to her.

'Why do you need me with you?'

'Because you're my last chance.'

And his mouth came down on hers.

She could hear a car pulling up beside them and Meg knew this was *her* last chance to get away. She knew instinctively that when the car doors opened she would be shoved in, that that was why he had taken the call—to arrange all this. Terrified, Meg did the only thing she could think of to survive. She bit hard on his lip with all she had—took that beautiful mouth and bit it as hard as she could. In the second when he recoiled, as he cursed her in Portuguese and reached for his gun, Meg ran—ran as she never had—ran and ran faster as she heard gunshots.

She kept running till rough arms grabbed her and pulled her down, slamming her to the ground. She felt her cheek hit the pavement and the skin leave her leg as she rose to run again, heard another volley of gunshots and looked behind her. She saw police cars screeching up. Whoever had shielded her from him had gone. Then she stared at the body on the ground and it was the only thing she could see.

'Niklas!' she screamed, and tried to run back to him, for she hated the man but it was agony to see him lying dead and riddled with bullets.

She could not stop screaming. Not even when other arms wrapped around her and her face was buried in rough prison denim and she smelt him again—not his cologne, but the scent of Niklas, her drug of choice, a scent that till now had been missing. She heard him saying over and over that she was safe, that he was here, that now it would all be okay, but she still did not believe it was him—until he lifted her face and she met his eyes, saw that the beautiful mouth had not been bitten and knew that somehow it was him.

That she was safe.

It was just her heart that was in danger again.

CHAPTER ELEVEN

MEG DID NOT get to see him again. Instead she was taken to a police station. There were press clamouring outside as she was taken in to give a statement, and while she was waiting for a translator Rosa arrived.

Meg gave her statement as best she could. They kept talking about twins, and although she had already worked that out when she was being held in Niklas's arms, her brain was so scrambled and confused that even with a translator she could hardly understand the questions, let alone answer them.

Every time she closed her eyes she saw Niklas—or rather the man she had thought was Niklas—lying there dead. The raw grief and panic, the *knowing* in that moment that she would never see him again, that the man she had fallen so heavily in love with was now dead, was not a memory or a feeling she could simply erase.

Fortunately Rosa had told the police she would return with Meg tomorrow, but that for now she needed peace, and thankfully they accepted that.

'We will return at ten tomorrow,' Rosa told her.

They stepped out into the foyer and she saw him standing there, still dressed in prison denim. He took her in his arms and she knew then that she had to be careful, because the one thing she had worked out before this embrace was that she wasn't strong around him—that she'd only been able to break up with Niklas when it hadn't actually been him.

'I'm still angry with you.'

'I thought you might be.' He kissed her bruised cheek and didn't let her go as he spoke. 'We can row in bed.'

Which sounded a lot more like the Niklas she knew. He held her tight and pressed his face into her hair and she could feel his ragged breathing. For a moment she thought he was crying, but he just held her a moment longer and spoke into her hair.

'The press are outside so we have to go out the back. I am taking you far away from here. I need to stay in the city, but—'

'Não,' Rosa said.

Meg heard the word *amanhã* again, and realised Rosa was telling him that Meg must return to the police tomorrow.

'I'll ring Carla, then.'

With his arm still around Meg he took Rosa's phone and started to dial the number. Whilst he was occupied Meg stepped out of his embrace, and a little later, when they climbed into a waiting car, she sat on the back seat far away from him, needing some time alone.

Even though they went out the back way the

press still got some photos and it was horrible. They scrambled over to the car and blocked their exit, but the driver shook them off. Niklas told her it might be like this for a while, and that he was taking her to a hotel. He saw the start in her eyes.

'We're not going back *there*—I've asked Carla to book us into a different one.'

Us.

So easily he assumed.

They entered the new hotel the back way too, and were ushered straight to a waiting lift where Niklas pressed a high number. They stood in silence till Meg broke it.

'Did you get off?'

'I've been released on bail.'

'So why are you still wearing…?' And then she shook her head, because she was simply too tired for explanations right now.

They stepped out of the lift and there was hotel security in the corridor—'For the press,'

Niklas said, but it felt a lot like prison to her, and no doubt to him too, but he said nothing, just swiped open a door, leading her into a plush suite.

Meg stood there for a moment, only knowing for certain the city she was in and that Niklas was alive. She remembered her feeling at seeing him dead, and the fear that had gripped her in the moments before, and started shaking.

'I wanted to take you away from the city tonight, but because we need to go back to the police station tomorrow it is better that we stay here. I've had your stuff packed up, but it is in the other place…you'll have to make do for now…'

It was hardly 'make do'; there was food and soon she would take a bath, and then she sat and had a strong coffee. Niklas offered her *cachaca*—the same drink she had been offered a little while ago—and she shuddered as she remembered. He opened the fridge and opened a bottle of champagne instead.

Which seemed a strange choice and was a drink she hadn't had it in almost a year.

Not since their wedding.

It was the drink they had shared on the day they had met, and he poured her a glass now, kissing her forehead as they chinked glasses and celebrated that somehow they were both here. It was a muted celebration, and there was still so much to be said, but Niklas dealt with the essentials first.

'You need to ring your parents.'

'I don't know what to say to them,' Meg admitted. She felt like crying just at the thought of them, was dreading the conversation that had to be had—and how much worse it was going to be now, after not telling them anything.

'Tell them the truth,' Niklas said. 'A bit diluted.' He nudged her. 'You need to speak to them now in case they hear anything on the news, or the consulate might contact them. Have they tried to ring *you*?'

'I didn't even bring my phone with me,' Meg said.

'It will be at the other hotel,' Niklas said. 'For now they just need to know you are safe. I will speak to them if it gets too much.'

'No.' She shook her head—not at phoning them, but at the thought of him talking to them. She knew how badly things were going to go. 'I'll do it…'

'Now.'

'I still don't really know what happened.' But she took the phone, because he was right. They needed to know she was safe. 'Leave me,' she said, and was glad that he didn't argue.

Niklas headed into the bedroom and she dialled the number, then looked out of the window to a very beautiful, but very complicated city. She held her breath when she heard the very normal sound of her mum.

'How's Brazil?' Ruth asked. 'Or is it Hawaii this week?'

'Still Brazil,' Meg said, and because Ruth was her mum straight away she knew.

'What's wrong?'

It was the most difficult of conversations. First she had to tell her how Vegas had been and how she had married a man she had only just met. She diluted the story a lot, of course—an awful lot—but she still had to tell them how, the morning after their wedding, Niklas had upset her, how she had been trying to psyche herself up to divorce him.

And her mum kept interrupting her with questions that her father was shouting—questions that weren't really relevant because they still didn't know half of the story. So she told them she was here to visit him, that he had been arrested a while ago, but was innocent of all charges. Her mother was shouting and sobbing now, and her dad was demanding the phone, and they were simply getting nowhere, and then Niklas was back and she was so glad to hand the phone over to him.

She found out for certain then just how brilliant he was, how clever he was with people, for somehow he calmed her father down.

'My intention when I married your daughter was to take proper care of her. I was on my way to tell you the same when I found out that I was being investigated.'

He said a few more things, and she could hear the shouts receding as he calmly spoke his truth.

'I was deliberately nasty to her in the hope she would divorce me—of course she was confused, of course she was ashamed and did not feel that she could tell you. I wanted to keep her away from the trouble that was coming— in that I failed, and I apologise.'

They didn't need to know all the details, but he told them some pertinent ones, because as soon as they hung up they would be racing to find out the news for themselves. So he told them about the shooting, but he was brief and matter-of-fact and reiterated that Meg was safe. He told them that they could ring any time with more questions, no matter the time of day or night, and that he would do his best to answer them. Then he handed the phone back to Meg.

'You're safe,' her mum said.

'I am.'

'We need to talk…'

'We will.'

When she hung up the phone she looked at him. 'You could have told me the truth that day.' She was angry that he hadn't.

'What? Walk back in and tell you that I am being investigated for fraud and embezzlement? That the man you met twenty-four hours ago is facing thirty-five years to life in jail…?' He looked at her. 'What would you have said?'

'I might have suggested you didn't go back till you found out the case against you…' she flared. 'I might not be the best one in the world, but I *am* a lawyer...'

'My own lawyer was telling me to get straight back.' He kicked himself then, because had he confided in her—had he been able to tell her—he might not have raced back, might have found out some more information before taking a first-class flight to hell.

'I had to return to face it,' Niklas said. 'Would you have stood by me?'

'You never gave me that chance.'

'Because that was what I was most afraid of.' He was kneeling beside her and she could hear him breathing. 'You never asked if I did it.'

'No.'

'Even when you visited...even when you rang...'

'No, I didn't.'

'Did you believe I was innocent?'

'I hoped that you were.'

'There was too much love for common sense,' Niklas said.

She sat there for ages and was glad when he left her alone and headed to the bathroom. She heard his sigh of relief as he slipped into the bath water and thought about his words—because while she had hoped he was innocent, it hadn't changed her feelings towards him and that scared her. After a little while she wandered in to him.

'I am so sorry.' He looked at her. 'For everything I have put you and your family through.'

'It wasn't your fault.'

'No,' he said. 'But still, I have scared you, and nearly cost you your life...'

And then he looked at her and asked the question the police had asked her earlier.

'Did he do anything to you?'

'Apart from hold a gun at me...' she knew what he meant '...no.'

She watched him close his eyes in relief and knew then that he *had* cried.

'He wanted to walk,' Meg said. 'That was when I started to worry.' She gave him a pale smile. 'Not quite the Niklas I know.' And then there wasn't a pale smile. 'I'm still cross about what you said on the phone.'

'I wanted you to leave,' he said. 'I wanted you to be so angry, so upset, that you got on the next plane you could…'

'I nearly did.'

'Do you want me tell you what happened?'

She wanted to hear it now, and he held his hand out to her. Yes, he assumed she would join him—and for now he was right. Her clothes and her body were filthy, and she wanted to feel clean again, to hear what had happened, and she wanted to hear it as she lay beside him. So she took off her clothes and slid into the water, with her back to his chest, resting on him, and he held her close and washed all her bruises and slowly he told her.

'There was bedlam in court,' Niklas said as he washed her gently. 'The place erupted when I asked for a new lawyer, and then Rosa presented the evidence implicating Miguel. He was arrested immediately, but of course I had to go back to prison...I knew they were never going to release me just like that. I told them that you were in danger, but they would not listen, and then, as they were taking me back, *he* made contact with Carla, asking for money. He said that he had my wife and texted a photo. The police only believed me then that I had a twin.'

She frowned and looked up to him. 'You *knew* you had a twin?'

'I guessed that I did last night, after I spoke to you.'

'How?'

'It made sense. I knew I was innocent.'

'But how did you work it out?'

'I swear in several languages…' She smiled, because that *was* what he did. 'I was angry after speaking to you—worried that you would not leave—and I swore in Portuguese. The guard warned me to be careful, he called me Dos Santos and I heard the derision in his voice, in his tone. I thought he was referring to me having no one, and I swore again, and then he said something about you. I went to curse again, but in Spanish…'

He was soaping her arms and his mouth was at her neck—not kissing, just breathing.

'The first nun who looked after me, till I was three, she taught me Spanish…'

Still Meg frowned.

'Dos Santos means something different in Spanish,' Niklas explained. 'In Portuguese it means "from the saints", in Spanish it means…'

'Two.' She turned and looked to him. '"Two saints".'

'There were two of us… That is why the

Spanish nun chose our surname. It made sense. Apparently in the month before I was arrested I was having meals and meetings with very powerful people, persuading them to invest....'

'My God!'

'He and Miguel were rorting every contact I have made. A couple of months before it happened I thought I had lost my phone, but of course they had it and were diverting numbers. Both of them knew that they didn't have long before I found out, or the banks or the police did, so they were busy getting a lot of money based on my reputation. My lawyer had every reason to want me to be convicted and spend life in jail—every reason not to tell me about the evidence that would convict me. Because as soon as I saw it, I would know the truth. It was not me.'

She felt him breathe in deeply.

'I can see how people were fooled. When I saw him lying there I felt as if I was looking at me.' He elaborated on his feelings no more than that, and told her the little he knew. 'His name was Emilios Dos Santos. The police said he had lived on the streets all his life but had no criminal record—just a few warnings for begging. I guess he was tired of having nothing. When he found out Miguel had been arrested he must have seen you as his last chance to get money from me...'

'How did he know I was here? How did he know what hotel...?'

'The prison guards, maybe.' He shrugged. 'Miguel would have been paying someone to keep an eye on me. You would have had to give your address for the prison visitors' list.'

She knew then how dangerous it had been not to listen to him, not to leave when he had told her to.

'I should have gone to Hawaii.'

'Yes,' he said, 'you should have.' But then he thought for a moment. Because without her here, without his fear that she was in danger, he might not have worked things out.

'It doesn't matter anyway,' Meg said. 'It's over now.' He didn't answer, and she turned and saw the exhaustion and agony still in his face. She could have kicked herself, for at the end of the day he had lost his twin, and Meg knew that despite all that had happened it had to hurt.

'Maybe he did want to talk to you when he found out he had a twin—perhaps Miguel dissuaded him, saw the chance to make some serious money and told him it was the only way.'

'I don't want to speak about that.'

So quickly he locked her out.

And then the phone rang—trust the hotel bathroom to have one.

Niklas answered it.

'It's your father.' He handed it to Meg, and she spoke with her parents. Neither shouted this time, just asked more questions—and, more than that, they told her how much they loved her, and how badly they wanted her to come home as quickly as possible.

She was glad she was facing away from him, but glad to be leaning on him as they spoke and he held her. Later her father asked to speak with him, and he held out his wet hand for the phone and listened to what her father was saying.

'We have to give some more statements to the police, so Meg needs to be here for a few more days,' he said, 'but I will take her somewhere quiet.' He listened for a moment and then spoke again. 'She's tired now, but I will see what she wants to do in the morning, once she has spoken to the police.'

And then he said goodbye, and she frowned because they almost sounded a little bit friendly.

'He's coming around to me.'

It was, as Meg knew only too well, terribly easy to do so.

'They want you home, Meg.'

'I know that, but I want to be here with you.'

'Well, they need to see you,' Niklas said. 'They need to see for themselves that you are not hurt.'

'I know that…' She wanted him to say he'd come with her, wanted him to say he would never let her go, but he didn't. She wanted more from him, wanted to be fully in his life, but still he would not let her in.

She turned her head and looked at him—looked at this man who'd told her from the start that they'd never last.

'This doesn't change things, does it?'

He didn't answer.

She surprised herself by not crying.

'You'll never find another love like this.' She meant it—and not in an arrogant way—because even if he didn't accept it, even if he refused to believe it, whether he wanted it or not, this really *was* love.

'I told you on the first day that it would not be for ever.'

'We didn't love each other as much then.'

'I have never said that I love you.'

'You did earlier.'

'I said there was too much love for common sense,' Niklas said. 'Too much love for you to think straight…'

'I don't believe you.'

'Believe in fairytales if you want to.' He said it much more nicely than last time, but the message was the same. 'Meg, I told you I could never settle in one place, that I could not commit to one person for ever. I *told* you that.'

He had.

'And I told you that I don't do love.'

He had.

'You said you wanted this for as long as it lasted.'

His voice was the gentlest and kindest she had heard it.

'In a few days, once all the questioning is over, you need to go home to your family.'

And even if she'd promised herself not to cry she did a bit, and he caught her tear with his thumb before lowering his head and tasting it. She could hear the clock ticking, knew that every kiss they shared now might be their last, that soon it would be a kiss goodbye.

'It could last...' She pulled her head away and opened her mouth to argue, but he spoke over her.

'I don't want to wait for the rows and the disenchantment to kick in. I don't want to do that to us because what we have now is so good. But, no, it cannot last...'

Which was why she'd accept his kisses—which was why, tonight, she would shut out the fact that this was temporary. Because tonight maybe she just needed to escape, and maybe he did too.

And even if he wouldn't admit it, even if he chose not to share his feelings, Niklas felt as if he'd just stepped out of hell's inferno into heaven as his mouth met hers.

Her mouth was bruised, but very gently he kissed it. Her cheek was hurting and her legs were grazed where she'd fallen. She knew she could never keep him, that for now guilt and fear would drive his kisses, and that later this man she didn't really know would return to a life she had never really been in. This wasn't love they were making. It was *now*.

Over and over she told herself that.

She thought he'd make love to her in the water, but he took her wet to the bed and dried her with a towel, every inch of her, and then he kissed her bruises, up her legs, and he kissed her *there* till she was crying and moaning in frustration. His hand was over her mouth again, because there were still guards outside, but she wanted him—wanted all of him. Then he slipped inside her, and it was incredibly slow, a savour in each thrust, but the words she needed were not in her ears. She bit down as she came, and gave him her body while trying to claim back a heart this man didn't want but already had.

CHAPTER TWELVE

MEG WOKE IN the night, crying and scared, and Niklas held her tightly before he made love to her again.

And he would have had her again in the morning—was pulling her across the mattress when the phone rang to tell them that Rosa was on her way up.

'Later!' he said, and kissed her. 'Or just really, really quickly now?'

She looked into black eyes that smiled down at her and simply could not read him—couldn't be his sex toy any more.

'Later,' Meg said, and climbed out of bed.

She let Rosa in. She had brought fresh clothes for both of them. Surprisingly, she gave Meg a hug and told her that she would accompany them to the police station.

'I am very sorry for the way I spoke to you,' Rosa said.

'What way?' Niklas checked.

She looked at Niklas. 'I gave her a hard time.'

'You weren't the only one,' Meg said, and then went purple when Rosa laughed. God, was that the only place minds went in Brazil? 'What I meant,' she said in her best cross voice, 'was that I do understand why you said what you did.'

'I am grateful,' Niklas said to Rosa. 'To all three of you, but especially to you. I will repay you just as soon as I get my assets back.'

'Hopefully it won't be long now,' Rosa said, and then smiled as she scolded, 'But did you *have* to drink the most expensive champagne in the fridge? I just paid your room bill.'

'*You* paid?' Meg blinked. She wasn't talking about the champagne. 'That was your money?'

Meg had assumed it came from Niklas's funds, but of course she now realised that while he was being investigated they would all be frozen.

'I put up my home,' Rosa said. 'I believed in him.'

'You're the richest one of us in the room,' Niklas said to Meg, and even Rosa laughed.

'I'll buy you all a coffee on the way to the station.' Meg smiled, but it was strained. She headed to the bathroom to get changed and thought about Rosa's belief in Niklas. It was clear to Meg that in the past Rosa and Niklas had slept together, but it wasn't that fact that riled her. It was the friendship they had that ate at her—a friendship that would not waver, one that would always last.

It was the longevity that riled her.

Meg opened the bag of fresh clothes and noticed that Rosa had chosen well for her. There was a skirt that was soft and long and would cover the grazes on her legs, a thin blouse and some gorgeous, albeit completely see-through, underwear. Meg inspected the underwear more closely and saw that there wasn't an awful lot of it, and when she pulled the knickers on she was silently mortified to realise that there was a hole in the middle—which was intentional. They were the most outrageous things she'd ever worn, but she could hardly complain to Rosa.

There were sandals too, because hers had broken yesterday.

She dressed and brushed her teeth, and combed her hair, and looked in the mirror and examined her solemn face. She should be happy and celebrating, except she couldn't quite rise to it. Memories of yesterday were still too raw, and she didn't understand how Niklas and Rosa could be smiling and chatting.

Didn't understand how Niklas could just turn his pain off.

But she had to learn how to, because soon she had to go home.

Had to.

She could not hang around and watch as his guilt for what he had put her through and the attraction he clearly had for her faded. She couldn't bear the thought of his boredom setting in as she waited for the news that she was to be dismissed from his life.

If Niklas didn't want for ever, then she couldn't carry on with it being just for now.

'Ready?' Niklas checked, looking over as she walked out of the bathroom.

'I guess so.' There was nothing to pack, after all.

'Do you want me to take your clothes and have them cleaned?' Rosa offered.

'I'll bin them.' Meg headed back to the bathroom to do so. 'I never want to see them again.'

'Okay.' Rosa hitched up her bag and headed off. 'I'll go and make sure the car is ready.'

When she'd left Meg picked up all the clothes from the wet bathroom floor and took them through to the bin in the lounge, but as she went to throw them in he stopped her.

'Not those.'

She looked at the denims he was retrieving and he turned and smiled.

'You might want me to shave my head again one day…'

She wasn't smiling back.

'It's all a game to you, isn't it?'

'No, Meg.' He shook his head, and he wasn't smiling now. 'It's not.'

But as they took the lift down she noted that he was holding a bag. He hadn't binned the denim clothes he'd worn in prison.

He pulled her into him and shielded her from the press as they left the hotel, did it again when they got to the police station, but she was actually shielding herself from him. He gave her a thorough kiss before she headed in to give her statement, but all it did was make her want to cry, because she wanted more than just sex from him.

'You'll be fine.' He wiped a tear with his thumb. 'Just tell them what happened. Rosa will be there…'

'I know.'

'It's nothing to be scared of,' he said. 'And then I'm going to get you right away from here—just us…' He smiled as he said it, gave her another kiss to reassure her.

She returned neither.

The statement was long and detailed, and she felt as if she were going over and over the same thing.

No, she had never met Miguel, and nor had Emilios mentioned him.

She didn't know who had called Emilios, but it had been after that call that he had suggested they go for a walk.

'They ask,' Rosa said, 'when did you realise it was not Niklas?'

'I never realised,' she said again.

'But you said you started to panic long before you saw the gun?'

She nodded, but Rosa told her she had to answer. 'Yes.'

They made her go over and over it, and she tried to explain things but it was so hard. It was hard to understand herself. She didn't want to say in the police station that she was surprised he hadn't taken her to bed, that perhaps that had been the biggest clue that it wasn't Niklas—which for Meg just rammed home how empty their relationship really was.

'So what made you panic?' Rosa checked again.

'I realised what a mistake I'd made marrying him,' Meg said, in a voice that was flat as she relived it. 'That there was no real basis for a relationship, that he'd always said it wouldn't last. All I wanted was to be away from him.'

'From Emilios?'

She shook her head. She remembered her swollen eyes and flinging things in a suitcase, the pleasure and pain of the last year, mainly the pain, and still, *still* he delivered it.

'From Niklas.' As she said it she saw Rosa's slight frown.

And then they took her further back, to her first meeting with Niklas on the plane and their late-night conversation.

'I asked how he'd been orphaned and he said he wasn't sure.'

'You asked if he had ever tried to look for his family?'

'Yes.'

'And what was his response?'

'He said that he had got Miguel, his lawyer, onto it, but he had got nowhere.'

'He said that?' the police officer checked via Rosa. 'He definitely said that?'

'Yes.'

The officer looked long and hard at her, and then Rosa asked if Meg was sure, as this was from a conversation a year ago. 'He asks if you are sure this is not the conversation you had with Niklas last night.'

Meg blinked.

'I told the police.'

'You remember this conversation exactly?' the officer checked, and she said yes, because she had been replaying every second of their time over and over for close to a year now.

'Exactly.' She nodded. 'And then I asked what it had been like, growing up in an orphanage, but he didn't respond,' Meg said. 'He told me he didn't want to speak about that sort of thing.'

But the police weren't interested in that part. Only Meg was.

She went over and over everything again. She

said that, no, she hadn't been aware she was being followed at the time, and looked to Rosa for explanation, but she gave a brief shake of her head. Then her statement was read back to her. She listened and heard that basically they had had an awful lot of sex and just a few conversations, but he had definitely mentioned that he had asked Miguel to look for his family. She signed her name to it.

'That is good,' Rosa said as they walked out. 'You have a good memory. They will jump on that part in court if Miguel denies that he was asked to find Niklas's family,' she warned. 'Just stay with that.'

'Am I free to fly home?' Meg asked. She saw the brief purse of Rosa's lips. 'My family's worried about me.'

'It might be better for Niklas's case if you were here.'

'What case?' Meg asked. 'It's clear he's innocent.'

'To you,' Rosa said. 'And it is to me. But dead men can't speak.' She gave a thin smile. 'I correct myself. When I said that Niklas never makes mistakes, he has made one—he hired Miguel, and he is a brilliant lawyer. He might say it was both of them that were conning people. He might insist he believed it was Niklas giving him instructions, or that the directions came from both of them...'

'No!'

'Yes,' Rosa said. 'I will fight it, but it might look better for Niklas if his wife was here beside him—not back home, counting the money his legal team has placed in her account.'

'You know it isn't like that.'

'Tell the judge,' Rosa said, and she was back to being mean. 'I get that your family is worried about you, but if you can pretend for a little while longer that Niklas is a part of your family...'

'Niklas doesn't want me to,' Meg retorted. 'Niklas doesn't want a family…'

'He doesn't even know what one is!' Rosa shouted. 'Yet he has done everything right by you.'

'Everything *right* by me?' It was Meg who was shouting now. 'Are we talking about the same man?'

It wasn't the best choice of words, given the circumstances—especially as Niklas appeared then.

'My mother had triplets, maybe?' he quipped.

It was her poor choice of words, perhaps, but his response was just in bad taste. She did not understand how he could be so laid-back about it. How could he have his arm around her and be walking out of the police station as if the nightmare of the last year hadn't even happened?

It was the same circus of cameras as before, and then they left Rosa to give the press a statement. A car was waiting for them. It's driver handed the keys over to Niklas, who sat behind the wheel as Meg sat in the passenger seat. The moment she was seated Niklas accelerated away at speed—away from the crowds of press. After a while the car slowed, and the drive was a long one, taking them out of the city and through the hills. There was little conversation, just an angry silence from Meg, whereas with every mile the car ate up Niklas seemed more relaxed.

'You're quiet,' he commented.

'Isn't that what you want me to be?'

Sulking didn't work with Niklas. It didn't bother him a bit. He just carried on driving, one hand on the wheel, the other out of the window. Any minute now he'd start whistling, just to annoy her further. She was still bristling from Rosa's words. The first thing she would do when she got back to Sydney was send back all the money that she had been paid.

He looked over at her tense profile. 'We'll be there soon.'

She didn't answer him.

Nothing made sense: the policeman's questions had confused her, Rosa had angered her, and as for him… She turned and could not fathom how calm he was after all that had happened. He was fiddling with the sound system now, flicking through channels. She did not need background music, and her hand snapped it off.

'The police said I was being followed. That it wasn't the police who shot him…'

'It was a bodyguard.'

'Bodyguard?'

'Just leave it.'

'No,' Meg snapped. 'I will not.'

'He will not do any prison time. I have my lawyers working for him. I had a couple of people following you when I realised you were still here—when I guessed I had a twin. I did not know exactly what was happening, but I knew you would not be safe, so I arranged to have people protect you.'

'How?'

'I owe a favour to a very powerful man,' Niklas said. 'He got a message to the outside after you rang me.'

And then he stopped talking about it, and she felt his hand come to rest on her leg, and she could not understand how easily he dismissed the fact that it was a bodyguard *he* had arranged who had shot his twin.

Did nothing get to him?

He gave her thigh a squeeze, which she guessed meant they were nearly at their destination and would be off to look at another bedroom any time soon.

'We're here.'

It was the most stunning house she had ever seen, with dark wood, white furniture and screens on the windows so the sun and the sounds of the mountains could stream in. It was gorgeous and, Niklas said, the place he had dreamt of when he was on the inside.

'You like it?'

'It's gorgeous.'

'Look...'

He took her by the hand and led her to the bedroom, then walked and opened huge glass doors, revealing lush grass that rolled towards another mountain. The sound of birds was all that could be heard. In a place like this, Meg thought, you could start to heal.

'There are servants, but I have told them not to come till I call them. They've left us lots of food...'

And there were her things, hanging in the wardrobe, and there were his arms around her, and again he was holding her close.

She started crying and he didn't seem surprised at all.

'You're exhausted,' he said.

She was.

From nearly a year of loving him.

'Are you about to suggest we go to bed?'

'Meg...' He saw her anger and he didn't blame her. 'I don't care how cross you are. You deserve to be. If you want to shout, go ahead. I have put you through hell and I am just trying to make you feel better, to say the right thing. I'm probably getting it wrong, but for now you are here, and safe.'

It was the 'for now' part that was killing her, but she wasn't going to go there again. 'I don't know what's wrong,' she said. 'I'm so angry! I'm so confused...'

'It's shock,' he said. 'You were nearly kidnapped. You saw a man shot.'

'I saw your *twin* shot!' she shouted. 'I thought it was you.'

He did not react—he just held her.

'Shouldn't it be the other way round?' She pulled away from him, so angry. 'Shouldn't *you* be the one crying? He was your brother.'

'That's for me to deal with,' Niklas said.

'Can't you deal with it with me?'

'I prefer to do things like that alone.' He was nothing if not honest. 'I don't want to talk about me. Right now I want to be here for you.'

He said all the right things, but they were the wrong things too. He took all of her, but didn't give himself back, and maybe she had better just accept it. He felt nothing for anyone, and as she looked out to the mountains she hoped here she might find a little peace before she left him.

'I hope the press don't find us here.'

'Not a chance,' Niklas said. 'I told you that.'

'If they know that you own it they soon will.' She looked down the mountain and hoped there were no cars loaded with press following them up, because she was beyond tired now, could not face moving again. She just wanted a moment to gather her thoughts. 'They'll be going through all your assets...'

'I don't own it,' Niklas said. 'It's not listed in

my assets. This is in your name…' He lifted up her face and kissed her frowning forehead. 'I bought this for you before I got arrested. I wanted the divorce, I knew I might be going away for a very long time, and this was to be part of your settlement. The sale went through the day before my finances were frozen…' He gave her a smile. 'They could not seize this because it is yours…'

'You bought this for me?'

'It is big enough for a bed and breakfast…' He shrugged. 'If that is what you want to do with it. I knew you would probably sell it…'

He had known he was about to be arrested and go to prison and yet he had still looked after her—had come to this place and chosen it. It was more than she could take in.

'Why are you crying?'

'Because of this.'

'I said I would take care of you.'

'And you have…'

He had kept every promise he had made, had listened to all her dreams.

They walked through the house and he showed her every room before he took her into the kitchen, with its massive ovens and benches, and huge glass doors that opened to let in the sound and the breeze of the mountains. He had chosen the perfect home—except he hadn't factored that he might live in it.

'I might have to stay here a while,' Niklas said. 'You can be my landlady.'

He came over for a kiss, because that was what he always did.

'I'll send you the rent I owe when I get it.'

'Send it?' Meg said.

'You need to go back.'

He did care about her. She knew it then—knew why he was sending her away. 'And you can't come with me.' It wasn't a question, she was telling him that she knew why.

He tried to hush her with a kiss.

'You can't come to Sydney even for a little while because you're still on bail.'

'Meg...'

When that didn't work, she was more specific. 'And you won't let me stay because you think you might go back to jail.'

'More than might,' Niklas said. 'Miguel is the best legal mind I have met...' He smiled. 'No offence meant.'

Always he made her smile, and always, Meg knew then, he had loved her—even if he didn't know it, even if he refused to see it. Rosa was right. He had always been taking care of her and he was trying to take care of her now.

'I'm on bail,' he said, 'and I doubt the charges will be dropped. Miguel will not simply admit his guilt. There will be a trial, there could be years of doubt, and then I might be put away again. You need to go back to your family.'

'*You're* my family.'

'No...' He just would not accept it. 'Because

as much as I might want you here, as much as I thought of you here in this home while I was in that place, as much as a three-weekly visit might keep me sane, I will *not* do that to you.'

'Yes.'

'No,' Niklas said. 'We will have a couple of nights here and then, as I promised your father, I will make sure you get home. By the time you are there I will have divorced you.'

He was adamant.

And she both loved and loathed that word now. She wanted to kiss the man she was certain now loved her, yet she wanted to know the man she loved. He kissed her as if he would never let her go, yet he had told her that she must.

'You're so bloody selfish…' She could have slapped him. She pulled her head back, would not be hushed with sex. 'Why don't I get a say?' She was furious now, and shouting. 'You're as bad as my parents—telling me what I want and how I should live my life…'

'What?' he demanded. 'You *want* to be up here, living in the mountains, coming to prison for a screw every three weeks?'

'Your mouth can be foul.'

'Your life could be,' Niklas retorted. 'Barefoot and pregnant, with your husband—'

She didn't hear the next bit. It was then that Meg remembered—only then that she remembered what she had been preparing to find out before Emilios had come to her door. He watched her anger change to panic, and in turn she watched the fear that darted in his eyes when she told him that she might already be.

It was not how it should be. Meg knew that.

He just stood there as she walked off, as she walked into the bedroom and went through her things. Yes, there was her toiletry bag and, yes, Rosa had packed everything. The pregnancy testing kit was there.

She kicked off her shoes when she returned to the kitchen, because barefoot and pregnant she *was*.

'You need to go home to your family.'

'That's all you have to say?'

'That's it.'

She couldn't believe his detachment, that he could simply turn away.

'You'd let us both go, wouldn't you?'

'You'll have a far better life…'

'I probably would,' Meg said. 'Because I am sick of being married to a man who can't even talk to me, who sorts everything out with sex. Who, even if he won't admit it, *does* actually love me. I'm tired of trying to prise it out of you.'

'Go, then.'

'Is that what you want?' Meg persisted. 'Or are you telling me again what I *should* want?'

'I could come out of this with nothing!'

And if Meg thought she had glimpsed fear before, then she had no idea—because now that gorgeous mouth was strung by taut tendons. His black eyes flashed in terror as he saw himself searching bins for food—not just for himself but for the family she was asking him to provide for. Meg knew then that she had never known real fear…would never know the depth of his terror.

She would not die hungry.

She would not leave the earth unnoticed.

She would be missed.

'I might not be able to give you anything…'

She glimpsed the magnitude of his words.

'We might have nothing.'

'We wouldn't have nothing,' Meg argued, with this man who had no comprehension of family. 'We'd have each other.'

'You don't know what nothing is.'

'So tell me.'

'I don't want to discuss it.'

'Then I *will* leave, Niklas, and I *will* divorce

you. And don't you dare come looking for me when the charges are dropped. Don't you dare try to get back in my life when you think the going can only be good.'

He just stood there.

'And don't bother writing to find out what I have, because if I walk out now I will do everything I can to make sure you can't find out. I will write "father unknown" on the birth certificate and you really will be nothing to your child.'

And she was fighting for the baby she had only just found out about, and the family she knew they could be, and as she turned to go Niklas fought for them too.

'Stay.'

'For what?' Meg asked. 'Shall we go to bed?' she demanded. 'Or shall we just do it here? Or...' she looked at him as if she'd had a sudden idea '...or we could talk.'

'You talk too much.'

He pulled her to him and kissed her mouth, running his hands over her, down her waist to her stomach. He pressed his hands into it for a second and then, as if it killed him to touch her there, he slid his hands between her thighs and moved to lift her skirt. He tried desperately to kiss her back to him, but she halted him and pulled her head away.

'And you don't talk enough.'

She would not let him go this time, and he knew he could not kiss her back into his life. And she *would* walk—he knew it. She was a thousand times stronger than she thought, and so must he be—for without her and his baby he was back to nothing.

'Don't waste time in fear, Niklas,' Meg said. 'You told me that.'

So he stood there and slowly and quietly told her what it had been like to be completely alone, to be moved on to yet another boys' home when he caused too much trouble, to boys' homes that had made living on the streets preferable.

And she *was* stronger than she'd thought she was, because she didn't cry or comment—just stood in his arms and listened. She'd asked for this, she reminded herself a few times at some of the harder parts.

'You would make a friend and then you would move on. Or he would steal from you and you would decide to go it alone. Then you might make another friend, and the same would happen again, or you would wake up and he would be lying dead beside you. But you keep on living, and you get a job, and it turns out you are clever—more clever than most—so you start to make money and you start to forget. Except you never do. But you make a good life for yourself, make new friends, and you would not change it, this new life, but still you taste the bitterness of your past. You make more money than you can spend because you're scared of having nothing again and, yes, you're happy—but it still tastes bitter.'

He didn't know how to explain it neatly, but he tried. He looked at her and could not fathom why she wanted to get inside his messed-up head.

'You never forget—not for one minute. You remember eating from bins and beatings, and running away, and the smell of sleeping on the streets, and you trust no one. You remember how people will take from you the second your back is turned—would steal from a beggar who sleeps on the streets. So you relish each mouthful you take and you swear you will never go back to being nothing. But always you fear that you will.'

And then he stopped.

'You want to hear the rest?'

'Yes.'

He paused, took a deep breath before continuing. 'Then you meet a woman on a plane, and this woman feels worried because in living her own life and following her dreams she might hurt her family, and you know then that there are people who do worry about others, who do care. And this woman changes your life.'

'I didn't.'

'More than that—you saved my life. Because when I did go back to having nothing I survived. More than I should have, I thought of you. Every night I saw the sun, and it was the colour of your hair. Then last night I got to hold you, and look back, and I realised that it is a good world. There are people you cannot trust, but there are also people you can—people who help you even if you don't know it at the time.'

She didn't understand.

'That a woman you only dated for a while would put up her house...' He hesitated. 'Rosa and I...'

'I worked that out.'

'It was before she was married, and there has

been nothing since, but her husband is still not pleased that she works for me. That she should go to him, that Silvio should trust her and me enough—that is real friendship,' he said. 'That does not let you taste bitterness.'

And that part she understood.

'Then you look back further and realise that the nun who taught you Spanish, the woman who named you, was the one good thing you can properly remember from your childhood and will end up saving the life of the woman you love—how can you not be grateful for that?'

'You can't not be.'

'And that woman you met on the plane—who your gut told you was right—who you married and then hurt so badly—would fly into Congonhas Airport to come and have paid sex with me...'

She thought of his anger in the prison, and the roughness of the sex, and then his tenderness afterwards, and she was so glad that he'd known he was loved, that she'd told him.

'I'd have done it for nothing.'

'I know,' he said, and he was honest. 'You loved me when I had nothing, and you will never properly appreciate what that means. But I might again have nothing, and I thought that was my worst nightmare, but to have nothing to give you or my child...'

'We've got a home that you chose for us,' Meg said. 'And I can work, and I have parents who will help me. Your child—our child—will never have nothing, and neither will you, so long as we have each other.'

He still could not really fathom it, but maybe he was starting to believe it.

'It might not mean prison...the charges could be dropped...' he said. 'Rosa thinks they have enough already to prove I was not involved. They are going through the evidence now.'

'And, unlike your wife, Rosa's got a good legal brain!' Meg said.

He didn't smile, but he gave a half-smirk.

'Rosa thinks it was Miguel who suggested the plan to my brother.' He tested this new thing called love. 'I want him to have a proper funeral. I want to find out more about him. I want to know about his life. Do you understand that?'

'Yes.'

'I might not talk about it without you.'

And still he said all the wrong things, but they were the right things for them.

'Whatever feels right for you.' And now she understood him a little better. She didn't have to know everything, didn't have to have all of him—just the parts that he chose to give. They were more than enough. And when he did choose to share, she could be there for him.

'Can you accept now that, even though I don't tell you everything, there are no secrets that might hurt you between us?'

'Yes.'

And then he did what Niklas did when he had to: he simply turned the pain of his past off. He smiled at her, held her, and then for the longest time he kissed her—a kiss that tasted deeper now, a kiss that had her burning.

But, unusually for Niklas, he stopped.

'And just to prove how much I love you,' he said, 'there will be no more sex for a while, so we can talk some more.'

'I didn't mean that.'

'No.' He was insistent. 'I can see what you were saying. We can go for a walk in the mountains.' He smiled and it was wicked. 'We can get some fresh air and we can talk some more...'

'Stop it.' His mouth had left her wanting.

She tried to kiss him, tried to resume, but Niklas shrugged her off and found a basket, started loading it from the fridge.

'We're going to have a picnic,' Niklas said. 'Is that romantic?'

He was the sexiest guy she had ever met, Meg realised, and she'd been complaining because they were having too much sex...

'Niklas, please.' She didn't want a picnic in the mountains, didn't want a sex strike from her Brazilian lover, and she told him so.

'Husband,' he corrected. 'I married you, remember?'

'Yes.'

'How can you say it was all about sex? I was nothing but a gentleman that day...I could have had you on the plane, but I married you first!'

'Hardly a gentleman,' she said. 'But, yes, you *did* marry me, and I get it all now. So can you put the basket down and...?'

'And what?' Niklas said.

Seemingly shallow, but impossibly deep, he was gorgeous and insatiable, and he was hers for ever.

His sex strike lasted all of two minutes, because now he was lifting her onto the kitchen bench even as he kissed her. His hands were everywhere and his mouth was too, but so were her hands before he slapped them away. '*I'm doing this.*'

He was the most horrible tease.

He whistled when he lifted up her skirt. 'What are you wearing?'

She writhed in embarrassment at his scrutiny. 'They're new.'

'You didn't buy these, though.' He smiled, because he couldn't really imagine his seemingly uptight girl buying knickers you didn't even have to take off.

'I might have.'

'Meg...' He was very matter-of-fact as he pulled down his zipper. 'You wore sensible knickers the day I met you. You even wore sensible knickers when you came to visit me in prison.' And then carefully he positioned her. 'Watch.'

And when he slipped straight into her the outrageous knickers she was wearing seemed like a sensible choice now.

'Never think I don't love you.' He would say it a hundred times a day if he had to. 'Never think that this is not love.'

And she knew then that he *did* love her, and that what they shared was much more than just sex. He was very slow and deliberate, and it was Meg who couldn't stop. He kept going as the scream built within her, and she waited for his hand to cover her mouth, waited for him to hush her—except they were home now, as he told her, and he pushed harder into her.

'We're home,' he said again, and moved faster, and for the first time she could scream, could sob and scream as much as she wanted, could be whoever and however she pleased.

And so too could he.

He told her how much he loved her as he came, and over and over he told her that he would work something out, he would sort this out.

And as he looked over her shoulder to the mountains he knew how lucky he was—how easily it could have been him lying dead on the pavement instead of his brother. His twin who must have tasted so much bitterness in his life too and been unable to escape as Niklas had done. When still he held her, when he buried his face in her hair and she heard his ragged breathing, for a moment she said nothing.

And then, because it was Niklas, he switched off his pain and came to her, smiling. 'Do you know what day it is today?'

'The day we found out we—' She stopped then, and blinked in realisation as her husband moved in to kiss her.

'Happy anniversary.'

CHAPTER THIRTEEN

SHE LOVED BRAZIL more and more every day she spent there, but it was the evenings she loved the most.

Meg lay half dozing by the pool, then stretched and smelt the air, damp from the rain that often came in the afternoon, washing the mountains till they were gleaming, and thought about how happy she was.

The charges had been dropped, but it had taken a couple of months for them to get back on their feet. They had paid Rosa back her money and lived off Meg's savings, but only when the nightmare of his returning to prison had stopped looming over them and Meg's pregnancy had started showing had Niklas really begun to think this was real.

There were now regular trips into São Paulo, and Niklas came to each pre-natal visit, and she loved that her family adored Brazil as much as Niklas did Australia when they were there.

She saw her parents often—they had only just left that day—and, thanks to a few suggestions and more than a little help from their new son-in-law, business was going well in Sydney.

They had surprised her—after the shock of finding out had worn off, they'd been wonderful. Niklas had flown them over to Brazil and the first day he'd met them he'd begun to work out why sometimes you couldn't just hang up the phone or shut someone out. He'd started to get used to both the complications and the rewards of family.

They hadn't shared their good news about Meg's pregnancy on that visit—it had seemed all too new and too soon to give them another thing to deal with, and there had also been a funeral to prepare for.

She had thought Niklas would do that on his own, except he hadn't.

Only a few other people had been invited. Meg had met Carla for the first time, and she was, of course, stunning, and there had been Rosa and her colleagues, and Rosa's husband Silvio too. And, even if they hadn't wanted to attend at first, her parents had come too, because they loved Meg and Niklas, and Niklas had told them how much it was appreciated. There had been flowers sent from Fernando—a fellow *paulistano* who knew only too well how tough it was on the streets, who knew that sometimes it was just about surviving.

Meg had been a bit teary, saying goodbye to her parents that morning, but they'd reassured her that they'd be returning in a month's time, so that they could be there for the birth of their grandchild.

If she lasted another month, Meg thought as

she felt a tightening again and picked up her baby guidebook.

No, it wasn't painful, and they were ages apart. So she read about Braxton Hicks for a while. But then another one came, and this time she noted the time on her phone, because though it didn't quite hurt she found herself holding her breath till it passed. Maybe she should ring someone to check—or just wait because Niklas would be home soon? It probably was just Braxton Hicks...

Her pregnancy book said so...

Meg loved being pregnant. She loved her ripening belly, and so too did Niklas. And she loved *him* more than she had thought she was capable of.

No, she'd never fully know him. But she had the rest of her life to try and work out the most complicated man in the world.

The nightmares had stopped for both of them

and life had moved on, and more and more she realised how much he loved her.

There was plenty of happiness—they had friends over often, and many evenings she got to do what she adored: trying out new recipes.

Meg looked at her phone. It had been ages since the last pain, so she should be getting started with dinner really. They had Rosa and her husband and a few other guests coming over tonight, to cheer Meg up after saying goodbye to her parents.

They had such good friends. She could even laugh at things now, and she and Rosa had become firm allies. Rosa would sometimes tease Meg about the earlier conversations they had shared—not to mention the outrageous knickers.

God, she'd been such an uptight thing then.

She lay blushing in her bikini at the thought of the lovely things they did, and then she felt another tightening. She looked at her phone again, noting the time. They were still ages apart, but as she heard the hum of the helicopter bringing Niklas home she was suddenly glad he was here. She walked across the lush grounds to meet him and picked a few ripe avocados from the tree to make a guacamole. As she did so she felt something gush.

It would seem the book was wrong. These weren't practice contractions, because there was real pain gripping her now—a tightening that had her blowing her breath out and feeling the strangest pressure.

Niklas saw her double over as he walked towards her. He could hear the chopper lifting into the sky and was torn between whether to ring and have the pilot return or just to get to her. He walked quickly, cursing himself because they had been going to move to his city apartment at the weekend, so that they could be closer to the hospital.

'It's fine...' He was very calm and practical

when he found her kneeling on the grass. 'I'll get the chopper sent back and we will fly you to the hospital. Let's get you into the house...' He tried to help her stand but she kept moaning. 'Okay...' he said. 'I will carry you inside...'

'No...' She was kneeling down and desperate to push—though part of her told her not to, told her it couldn't be happening, that she still had ages, must keep the baby in. And yet another part of her told her that if she pushed hard enough, if she just gave in and went with it, the pain would be gone.

'It's coming!'

She was vaguely aware of him ringing someone, and frowned when she heard who it was.

'Carla?'

She wasn't thinking straight, the pain was far too much, but why the *hell* was he calling Carla?

'Done,' he said.

'Done?'

'Help is on the way…'

She could see him sweating, which Niklas never did, but his voice was very calm and he was very reassuring.

'She will be ringing for the helicopter to come back and for an ambulance…'

He saw her start to cry because she knew they would be too late—that the baby was almost here.

'It's fine…' He took off his jacket and she watched him take out his cufflinks and very neatly start to fold up his sleeves. 'Everything will be okay.'

'You've delivered a lot of babies, have you?' She was shouting and she didn't mean to.

'No,' he said, and then he looked up and straight into her eyes, and he turned her pain and fear off, because that was what he did best. 'But I did do a life-skills course in prison…'

And that he made her smile, even if she was petrified, and then she started shouting again when he had the gall to answer his ringing phone.

'It's the obstetrician.'

She must remember to thank Carla, Meg thought as he pulled down her bikini bottoms. From what she could make out with her limited Portuguese he was telling the doctor on speakerphone that, yes, he could see the head.

She could have told the doctor that!

But she was sort of glad not to know what was being said—sort of glad just to push and then be told to stop and then to push some more. She was *very* annoyed when he said something that made the obstetrician laugh, and she was about to tell him so when suddenly their baby was out.

'*Sim,*' he told the doctor. '*Ela é rosa e respiração.*'

Yes, her baby was pink and breathing. They were the best words in the world and, given he had said *ela*, it would seem they had a baby girl.

The doctor didn't need to ask if the baby was

crying for it sang across the mountains—and Meg cried too.

Not Niklas—he never cried. Just on the day he'd found out she was safe she had seen a glimpse, and then the next day she had guessed he might have been, but he was in midwife mode now!

He did what the doctor said and kept them both warm. He took his shirt off and wrapped his daughter in it, and there was his jacket around Meg, and then he got a rug from beside the pool and covered them both with it. He thanked the doctor and said he could hear help arriving, and then he turned off his phone.

'She needs to feed,' he told her, and he must have seen her wide eyes. He was an expert in breastfeeding now, was he? 'The doctor said it will help with the next bit…'

'Oh…'

'Well done,' he said.

'Well done to you too.' She smiled at her lovely midwife. 'Were you scared?'

'Of course not.' He shook his head. 'It's a natural process. Normally quick deliveries are easy ones...'

He said a few other things that had her guessing he'd been reading her book—the bit about babies that come quickly and early.

'She's early...' Meg sighed, because she had really been hoping that this would be a very late baby, that somehow they could fudge the dates a little and she would never know she'd been made in prison.

'It will be fine,' he said. 'She was made with love. That's all she needs to know.'

They had a name for a boy and one for a girl, and he nodded when she checked that he still wanted it. She tasted his kiss. Then she saw him look down to his daughter and thought maybe she glimpsed a tear, but she did not go there— she just loved that moment alone, the three of them, just a few minutes before the helicopter arrived—alone on their mountain with their new baby, Emilia Dos Santos.

The Portuguese meaning, though.

From the saints.

* * * * *